A Pig Called Heather

Harry Oulton has worked for Eurodisney in Spain, Coca-Cola in Mexico, made television programmes for both the BBC and ITV, and worked in a factory sticking labels onto boxes. Now he's very happy writing children's books in London, where he lives with his wife and three children. Find out more at www.harryoulton.co.uk or follow him on Twitter @HarryOulton1

The HEATHER series

A Pig Called Heather
The Return of a Pig Called Heather
Heather's Piglets

A Pig Called Heather

HARRY OULTON

Piccadilly
PRESS

First published in Great Britain in 2014 by
PICCADILLY PRESS
80-81 Wimpole St, London W1G 9RE
www.piccadillypress.co.uk

Falkirk Council	
Askews & Holts	2015
JF JF	£5.99

The right of Harry Oulton to be identified as Author of this
work has been asserted by him in accordance with
the Copyright, Designs and Patents Act, 1988

incide ... and all incidents, places, events and ... are the product of the author's imagination or are used ... Any resemblance ... living or dead, or actual events is purely coincidental.

A CIP catalogue record for this book is
available from the British Library.

ISBN: 978–1–848–12472–1
also available as an ebook

1 3 5 7 9 10 8 6 4 2

Typeset in Adobe Caslon Pro 12.5/17pt

Printed and bound by Clays Ltd, St Ives Plc

Piccadilly Press is an imprint of Bonnier Publishing Fiction,
a Bonnier Publishing company.
www.bonnierpublishingfiction.co.uk

SCOTLAND

ABERDEEN

THE FORTINGALL YEW

GLASGOW

EDINBURGH

NEWCASTLE

HADRIAN'S WALL

ROUTES TAKEN:
Heather & Aitor
Eder & Tor

SHERWOOD FOREST

ENGLAND

WALES

CARDIFF

BRISTOL

LONDON

N
W E
S

0 20 40 60 80 100 M
0   40   80   120 160 K

For Curly

Chapter 1

Hats & Carrots

When the pig called Heather woke up after lunch, the first thing she thought was that she had absolutely nothing to do. That was good – doing nothing was one of her best things, and also one of the things she did best. So while she thought about doing nothing and how nice it was going to be, it occurred to her that doing nothing might be even nicer if you could think about nothing while you were doing it.

She went and found her best friends, Rhona the goat and Alastair the sheepdog.

'I'm off to the field.'

'What for?' asked Rhona.

'No reason,' replied the pig.

'What are you going to do?'

'Nothing.'

'Nothing?'

'That's right. Nothing.'

'Can we come?'

'I'd rather you didn't. It's easier to do nothing if you're on your own. I'm going to try and think about nothing as well.'

Of course, if you've ever tried to think about nothing, you'll know it isn't really possible, mainly because the moment you think you're thinking about nothing you realise that you are in fact thinking about something, even though that something is nothing. And that's exactly what Heather was thinking when two brand new thoughts barged into her head like envelopes through a letterbox.

Isla, and the shiny thing.

Isla was her best friend. Always had been. Best two-legged friend, that is. Heather could remember when Isla's mum was walking around with a huge tummy telling them all she was going to have a baby. Then Isla was born and was soon zooming around the farmyard on her bottom, wearing nappies and eating mud. She learnt to stand by using Heather's tail to pull herself up and then wobbling, one jammy hand on Heather's back and a triumphant grin on her face. She'd spent hours making Heather kneel down, like a camel, so that she could climb on her back and parade around the farmyard. Her first day at school, her panic when her first tooth fell out, her shout of triumph when she finally managed to climb the tree by the ruin, and her yelp of alarm as she fell off it.

There were bad memories too. In particular, the awful evening when Isla came running out of the house in floods of tears and hid in the corner of the barn with Heather, crying and crying because her mother had died. Isla stayed in the barn that night. Her dad came out to see her, but she said she didn't want to be in the house and he seemed to understand that. She clung to Heather all night, like a very large, very sweaty piglet.

After that she'd spent more and more time with Heather. Quite often she fell asleep in the barn and then her dad would come and carry her inside, fast asleep. Heather had seen her grow into this amazing little girl – thoughtful, naughty and so chatty! From the moment she'd said her first word – 'tractor' – she hadn't stopped talking.

So why had she not come to see Heather for two whole days? Something was wrong.

The shiny thing was right in the middle of her field, and it glinted every time the sun came out from behind the clouds and shone at it. What was it?

Heather went over to investigate. It was small and round, and although it was covered in earth it still managed to twinkle at her. She sniffed at it but it didn't smell of very much. She gingerly took a bite but it was very hard and tasted like blood so she spat it out again quickly. It was annoying though – she didn't like having something in her field that she couldn't either identify or eat. She could bury it again, but then she'd always know it was there. The answer came to her when she heard the familiar *thump, thump, thump* of Isla's skipping rope. Isla would know what it was. Isla was really clever. She always knew stuff like that. And maybe she could find out why Isla wasn't talking to her. Get rid of both thoughts at once. Then her head would be nice and empty again. Trying to avoid biting into it, she put the thing in her mouth and walked over to the gate that separated the field from the back garden.

Heather spat out the shiny thing and then put her trotters onto the top of the gate and oinked loudly. No response from the garden. She oinked again, louder. Still no response. Isla must have her iPod on. Heather sighed. She didn't like squealing, but it looked like she had no choice. She checked nobody important was listening, took a deep breath and squealed, just like a pig.

Isla looked up, grinned, got her feet all tangled up in the skipping rope and fell in a heap on the ground.

She picked herself up, unplugged her headphones

and ran over. 'Heather Duroc! There you are! I've been looking everywhere for you. Where were you?'

She was called Heather Duroc because she liked eating heather, and she was a Duroc pig. Her mother had been called Eggshells Duroc, her father Potatoes Duroc, one of her sisters had been named Yogurts Duroc, and her brother, after an unfortunate incident when the back door was left open and the kitchen unattended, had always been known as Chocolate Mousse Duroc.

'I've finally got Dad to agree that you can come to school with me tomorrow. I didn't want to get your hopes up so that's why I didn't say anything before, but tomorrow's pet day at school and Dad says I can take you! Not that you're a pet or anything, I mean, you're like a proper working animal, but because we're such good friends I asked Dad if it would be okay and he said yes. So tomorrow morning we'll get the school bus together and you can spend the whole day at school with me!'

School! Heather gulped and pushed her snout into Isla's hand so the little girl wouldn't realise how nervous she was. She didn't know what happened at school, although Isla seemed to do a lot of counting. She did say lunch was nice though, so it couldn't be all bad.

Heather remembered that she'd had something important to ask Isla, so she dropped to the ground, picked up the funny thing in her mouth and stuck out her tongue with the thing on it.

'Ooh, an old coin. That's pretty. Where d'you find it?'

'Isla, come on, love – it's teatime!' shouted Farmer Wolstenholme from over by the house.

Heather waved her snout back towards the middle of the field, but she wasn't sure if Isla registered.

'I've got to go now – Dad's calling me in. I'll come out and see you later.' She pocketed the coin, leant across the fence and whispered, 'Dad's done carrots for tea so I'll try and smuggle some out to you!'

That sounded promising and Heather snuffled contentedly as her friend raced across the farmyard to where her dad was waiting for her. She watched her fondly, amazed as always at the amount of energy contained in that little body with its spindly arms and bandy legs. Always on the move, always so excited about everything, always trying to squeeze even more juice out of the day. It made Heather feel tired just watching her. Maybe that was why they got on so well. Isla reminded Heather of one of her piglets, and as Heather couldn't answer her, Isla got to talk and talk without ever having to stop.

She was enjoying thinking about Isla, so she was extra cross when a strange van drove into the farmyard and parked a new thought in her head. The van was white and gold, and on top of it were perched three huge plastic chickens, bent over and with their wings out, looking like they were going to take off at any second.

'*Busby's Birds*. Must be a chicken farmer,' said Rhona, who had just arrived and was reading what was written on the side of the van.

A tall, angular man uncoiled himself from inside it like a snake being charmed out of a basket.

The man looked around him, nodded in a pleased fashion and reached for his mobile phone. He dialled and held it to his ear as he looked around him.

'I'm at the farm now. You were right, it's perfect.'

He listened for a bit, nodding all the time and then he smiled, his teeth white and gleaming. 'I've not seen the cellar yet, but if it's as big as you say it'll do us just fine.'

He hung up and walked over towards the farmhouse.

Heather was curious. 'What does he want? We're not a chicken farm.'

'I don't know,' replied Rhona, 'but that's a ridiculous name. Everyone knows a busby is a hat. Soldiers wear them. Like the ones who guard Buckingham Palace, where the Queen lives.'

'Doesn't the Queen wear a crown?' asked Heather, a bit confused.

'She does. It's how you know she's the Queen. But this man's a chicken farmer. Named after a hat. I don't like it. Or him.' She turned away gloomily. 'How are you, anyway?'

'Exhausted. Rhona, what exactly do you do at school?'

'Why?'

So Heather started to tell her about Isla and pet

day and together they headed off to the barn for their supper. The trough was full of delicious slops and Heather got stuck in straight away. For quite some time she was too busy eating to say anything, and then suddenly she stopped. Something very alarming had just occurred to her. She sat down on her haunches and looked so worried Rhona stopped eating and raised an eyebrow questioningly.

Heather swallowed. 'Do you think the hat man is staying for tea? Only, Isla promised me carrots. If he stays there may not be any left.'

Chapter 2

Pets
& Robbers

It was pet day and Isla and Heather were at the bus stop.

'Today's going to be so, so cool. This is the first year I've been able to bring in a pet for pet day because we've not had it because of foot and mouth. Miss Stephenson says it doesn't matter if we don't have anyone to bring, but all of us in my class have definitely promised that we're all bringing an animal in, even Tullynessle Morag and she hasn't even got a pet so she's going to borrow her neighbour's cat, although she says he's really old so he might be a bit freaked because it can get really noisy at school, so she thinks her mum might just make her catch a spider or something, because they can be pets too, like when Callum brought in his stick insect for show and tell, and we all tried to spot him in the case and it was really hard because he was green like a leaf and shaped like a stick so he completely impossible to find. And he didn't move. Camouflage. That's what Miss Stephenson said. She said it's like when you wear white things in the snow, or green things in the jungle, so that people can't see you. Callum said he could see him but I don't think there was anything in there at all. Just loads of sticks.'

The bus pulled up and they got on. Isla was still talking.

'... So Millie's probably my best friend. She's called Millie Raphael-Campbell because her dad's Scottish but her mum's mum was like this really cool South American Indian woman who lived by this huge river called the Amazon and it was miles from anywhere so she used to go to school on a boat! How cool is that? This is her stop. Look, she's got her chickens with her! Hi Millie, this is Heather, she's coming to school today.' She leant forward and whispered to her friend. 'I think she's a bit nervous so be nice to her.' Then she leant back again. 'You've got your chickens, that's so cool, what are they called? We're going to have the best day!'

Isla's friend had straight black hair, and when she grinned at Heather it made her eyes twinkle like an apple when the sun hits it. That thought made Heather's tummy rumble. 'Hi Heather, Isla talks about you all the time! It's so good you're red. All my cousin Mac's pigs are pink, except some of them have got black splodges, you know, because they're Saddlebacks.' Then she held up a big basket full of chickens and started introducing them. 'That's Tikka Masala, this one is Korma, that one in the corner's Tandoori, here's Butter and the speckled one's Biryani.

I was going to bring Karahi as well, but Mum wouldn't let me. Iain said he'd try and bring Daisy but you know what his dad's like, he's so protective he won't hardly let her out of his sight!'

Heather gulped. Millie talked even faster than Isla! If everyone at school talked that fast, how was she going to understand anyone?

The bus slowed down and turned into Old Meldrum School. It was a low, wide building with a high bit in the middle. Sort of shaped like Isla when she stretched her arms out and ran down the hill. The bus pulled up right where Isla's nose would have been and there was a loud hiss as the driver opened the door and everyone pushed and barged to get off. Heather stared out of the window and her heart sank again. There were people everywhere, all chatting, and they all seemed to know each other.

Isla was already off the bus, but Heather hadn't moved. She couldn't. She wasn't ready for this. Isla stuck her head back inside when she realised Heather wasn't with her.

'Come on, what you waiting for?'

But Heather was frozen. She couldn't get up from the seat.

Isla came back onto the bus and put her arm round her. 'Come on, we're here now, everyone's waiting.'

Heather sank further into the seat. Why was she here? She didn't belong here. She just wanted to go back to the farm.

The figure of the lady bus driver loomed over them as she looked down at the two friends. 'Will I take her back home, Isla pet?'

Isla shook her head at her, picked up the piece of string she'd tied around Heather so they wouldn't get separated, and gave it a little twitch. Then she reached into her pocket and pulled out an apple which she offered Heather. *Fall Pippin, tender flesh, rich flavour and excellent for eating.*

'I was saving this for you to have at breaktime, but I suppose you could have it now. If you get off the bus.'

Heather took a deep breath, scrunched her snout at her friend, slid off the seat and trotted off the bus after Isla, bravely chewing the delicious apple as she went.

Things improved quite a lot after that. As it was pet day at the school, there were loads of animals all standing around in the playground, some of them just as nervous as Heather. She quickly got chatting to a really old cat called Lola who'd been coming to pet day for years. She was here with her owner Tabitha, but as Tabitha had an older sister and a younger brother, Lola said she was always being dragged to a pet day or to show and tell. Then a very loud bell went and Isla led her inside.

All the children in Isla's class sat at their desks with their pets, and Miss Stephenson went around the room getting everyone in turn to stand up and introduce their pet. As so many of the children lived on local farms there was quite a collection.

'Raj, why don't you start us off?'

A small boy was sitting at the back of the class holding a sort of see-through plastic cage.

'This is my hamster, Derek. He's called Derek because a derrick is a type of crane that they use on oil rigs, so my mum said we should call him that so we'd remember my dad because he works on an oil rig. Derek's quite old now and he's a rubbish pet because he's nocturnal, which means he spends all day sleeping and only wants to play at night. Mum says I'm only allowed one pet though, so I really hope he dies soon so I can get a massive dog like a wolfhound or something.'

'Thank you, Raj.' The teacher smiled, and turned to a girl close to Isla. 'Karen?'

'This is my sheep, Donal. I've looked after Donal ever since he was born and his mammy died when she got stuck in a snow drift and my mum and dad didn't find her for three whole days. When they did she was totally dead and frozen stiff and she wouldn't fit into the quad bike trailer so Dad had to break her legs and saw through—'

'Thank you, Karen, that's lovely,' interrupted the teacher smoothly. 'Now who's next? Isla, who have you brought in today?'

Isla stood up and Heather sat up nervously on her haunches and looked at the sea of children gazing at her.

'Hi, you all know I live on a farm with my dad. It

used to be a pig farm, but my dad says there's no money in pigs these days, so last year he turned it into a barley farm instead. Heather is the last pig on the farm. She's a Duroc pig which is why she's red, and we've always been really good friends. Dad says when my mum died, Heather was really nice to me. He says it was like she knew how sad I was and she would sort of butt me with her head to make me feel better. We talk all the time, only she can't answer me so I tell her to scrunch. Like this, watch.'

She bent down and looked at Heather.

'Heather, would you like an apple? Scrunch if you do.'

What a ridiculous question, thought Heather. *Of course I want an apple. I always want an apple.* She scrunched her snout good and hard to make sure that everyone in the classroom realised that yes, she would like an apple extremely very much, please.

As she did, everyone laughed and cheered and Isla looked proud. 'Does anyone have an apple for her? Only I've already given her mine.'

Miss Stephenson opened her drawer and gave

Heather an apple. *Aromatic Russet, a high quality Russet with a rich flavour and a hint of lemon.* Heather munched happily and Isla sat back down at her desk.

Miss Stephenson looked around the classroom and spotted one boy on his own at the back. 'Iain? Have you not brought a pet in today?'

The boy looked surprised. 'Aye. Daisy. But she's a bit big to bring inside so my mum's got her in the playground.'

He leant out of the window. 'Say hello, Daisy,' he said, and was rewarded with a very loud *moo* from the playground.

There were cats, dogs, a snake, Millie's chickens, a rabbit and several spiders. Once they'd all been introduced, Miss Stephenson let everyone mingle and at lunchtime they all had picnics together in the playground. Then they all lined up with their pets for a group photo, which Miss Stephenson said she was going to enter in a competition to win a trip to the world famous London Zoo. With all that going on, Heather had such fun she forgot all about the time until Isla came to get her and told her that Millie's mum was going to give them a lift home.

Heather followed Isla back to the classroom and everyone started to get ready. And that was when the trouble started. Isla could see Millie looking more and more panicked as she frantically scanned the classroom.

'What's up?'

'I've lost Korma.'

'What do you mean?'

'I mean, where's Korma? Look, we've got Tikka Masala, there's Tandoori with Butter and here's Biryani, but we're missing Korma! She's the best layer. She did three double yolks last week. My mum's going to kill me!'

Isla ran off to get Miss Stephenson, and everyone set to work looking for the missing chicken. The gate to the schoolyard was closed to prevent escape and everyone was walking around shouting, 'Korma! Where are you? Here Korma Korma Korma!' and making funny clucking noises as they did. They turned the school upside down, but Korma was nowhere to be found.

When Millie's mum arrived and Millie told her what had happened she was furious, and poor Miss Stephenson looked like she was about to burst into tears.

'How can you have lost one of my chickens! Korma's the best layer on the farm!'

'I'm so sorry, Mrs Raphael-Campbell; I can't think where she can have got to.'

Heather was sitting with the other four chickens while they watched everyone searching and waited to go home.

'They want to try looking in that wee boy's ruckysack,' muttered one of the chickens.

Heather looked at her in confusion. 'Which boy? What? Why?'

'T'wasnae so bulgy when he came tae school this mornin'.'

'Aye. True enough,' added another of them with a gloomy nod.

Heather was horrified. 'What? You think he's . . . ?'

'Jimmy Jamieson. He's a wee devil. And his ma and pa run the Heart of Palm. Need I say anything else?'

Heather trotted over to where Isla was comforting a distraught Millie, bit her coat and tugged. Isla looked down at her.

'We can't go yet, we can't find Korma anywhere.'

Heather pointed her snout towards Jimmy, but Isla didn't register. She pulled on the hem of Isla's coat again and the little girl looked down.

'What is it?'

Heather waved her head sideways towards Jimmy. Isla looked at the boy closely. She knew Heather was trying to tell her something, but what could it be? At that point Jimmy's mum came into the playground and went over to Miss Stephenson.

'Some of us have got better things to do than wait around here all day because you're too dippy to look after a few animals. I'm taking him home and I'll see you in the morning.'

Miss Stephenson nodded sadly. As Heather watched in alarm, Jimmy picked up his bulging rucksack and headed out of the school gate after his mother.

She had to do something! She took a deep breath,

gathered herself and, with no idea what she'd do when she got there, charged after the departing Jimmy, oinking loudly as she went.

'Jimmy! Look out!' called someone from behind her and Jimmy turned just in time to see a very large red pig galloping straight towards him. It was a frightening sight, but Jimmy was (unluckily for Heather) rather a good cricket player and, as Heather arrived, he took the bag off his back and swung it as hard as he could, as if she were a very large cricket ball.

Thwack! Heather felt like her head was going to explode as she rolled sideways over and over and over, the world spinning around so she kept seeing the sky and then swirling people and then the sky again. But the impact was too much for Jimmy's rucksack and it burst open. Almost in slow motion everybody watched the contents sailing through the air – school books, a water bottle, marbles, pens, a catapult, two un-matching socks, the remains of his packed lunch, but no chicken . . .

Chapter 3

Polar Bears
& Haunted Trees

'So he hadn't stolen the chicken?' asked Katy in disbelief. Katy was an Eider sea duck who came to the farm every year to have her babies. The animals enjoyed her visits because she had been all over the place and was always full of amazing stories about far-away places and incredible things from distant countries. The only trouble was, because she'd travelled all over the world and seen so many things, at times she could be a teeny bit boasty, and whatever you told her, she always seemed to have a better, more exciting story involving her adventures.

It was the evening and everyone was gathered in the barn listening to what had happened at school. They all liked the story so much that Heather had told it three times and she'd just got to the bit when the rucksack had burst open and Korma hadn't been hidden inside. Katy had been resting for the first two times so she hadn't heard and Heather was happily telling the story again.

'Oh he'd stolen her all right, he'd just hidden her in his mum's car. Isla guessed what had happened. She went to Jimmy's car and heard Korma clucking in the boot! Mrs Jamieson was so embarrassed when Isla opened the boot and let her out. Jimmy wasn't a bit ashamed. He said chicken korma was his favourite kind of curry and he wanted it for his tea.'

Everyone was laughing and begging Heather to tell it again, but Rhona wanted to hear about the other pets, so Heather started to tell them about

Callum's camouflaged stick insect, and that was when Katy interrupted.

'Of course, that's why I'm this mixed brown colour. It's so that predators can't see me easily. I was talking to a polar bear the other day who told me something amazing. Who knows the answer to this one? What is the colour of a polar bear's fur?'

Rhona tried to get Heather's attention, but Heather ignored her and shouted the answer.

'White! Polar bears are white! It must be their camouflage so they can hide in the snow!'

Katy smiled and fluffed her feathers to make sure she had everyone's attention.

'Wrong! That's a very common mistake. Actually polar bears have hollow fur. It reflects the light which makes them *appear* white. Their skin is actually black which helps them absorb the heat better as well. They're extraordinary creatures, and so interesting to talk to.'

As Katy droned on to the chickens, Heather trotted off feeling rather stupid and was sitting quietly on her own when Rhona came and found her.

'Don't feel bad. Most people would say polar bears have white fur.'

'You wouldn't.'

'But I read a lot. I know loads of useless stuff.'

'It's just she always makes me feel so boring. Like I never do anything. Why can't I travel the world and meet all these amazing creatures?'

'Pigs don't migrate. Well, apart from those funny bearded ones who live in Sumatra. They travel all over the place but they're a bit scary. Your life is here. You have plenty of adventures without having to leave the farm. She doesn't have Isla, does she?'

Rhona always knew the right thing to say and Heather was cheered up again.

'So what adventures have been happening while I've been at school?'

Rhona twitched her beard, something she always did when she was worried.

'Mr Busby's here again. This is the third time. Something very bad is going to happen, I think. It did cross my mind that he might even want to buy the farm.'

'Buy the farm? The hat man? But we're not for sale. Are we? Why didn't Isla tell me?'

'That's why I'm worried,' continued the goat. 'If Isla's not saying anything to you, that means she doesn't know. Which means her dad hasn't told her. He tells her everything; so if he doesn't want her to know, that means it probably isn't good news. So come on, we've got some investigating to do.'

Heather swallowed and followed Rhona over to the farmhouse. Rhona made her lie down and then she climbed onto Heather's back.

'Right, stand up, but slowly – it's a bit wobbly.'

Heather got onto her hind legs first and then her front ones.

'Good,' said the goat. 'Now, when I'm on your shoulders, sit back down on your haunches but keep your head up. Okay?'

Rhona put her front legs against the kitchen wall and balanced her back hooves on the pig's shoulders. Heather lowered her bottom, which pushed Rhona a bit higher, just high enough in fact to rest her hooves on the kitchen window ledge and peer inside.

Heather was a bit puzzled. 'What are we doing?'

'Alastair's keeping watch, I'm eavesdropping.'

'E-whatting?'

'Eavesdropping. Listening in to someone's conversation without them knowing. Spying.'

'What am I doing?'

Rhona adjusted her feet on Heather's shoulders. 'You're providing invaluable support.'

Heather grunted. If she strained her head sideways she could see the pear tree that grew outside Isla's bedroom. Although she preferred apples, she was quite fond of a nice, crunchy Bartlett pear and there was a particularly juicy one glinting in the moonlight, teasing her with its plump perfection. It was still attached to the tree, but it was so close to falling that it was bending the branch nearly in half, pulling down so hard on its stalk that it looked like it might uproot the entire tree! There was something cruel about it hanging just out of reach, and Heather tore her eyes away from it crossly, her tummy rumbling loudly as she did so.

'Shh,' said Rhona from her perch on Heather's shoulders. 'I'm trying to listen.'

Inside the kitchen, the skinny, white-toothed Mr Busby was sitting opposite Farmer Wolstenholme and drinking down a tall glass of milk. Farmer Wolstenholme had a leathery, wrinkled face which looked like one day he'd been laughing really hard and the wind had changed and left him with a permanent twinkle. Right now though, he was looking a bit worried as he listened to the man opposite him.

'Just hear me out, Anthony. You say you don't want to sell to me, but I really want to buy this place, and I always end up getting what I want. You mark my words, within six months' time I'll be sitting here and this will be my farm. Just accept it. It's inevitable.'

'Inevi-what?' asked Heather outside.

'Inevitable,' answered Rhona. 'Means you can't escape it. Now shush, I've got to listen.'

Back inside, Farmer Wolstenholme took a swig from his glass of water.

'But I'm just about to bring in the barley. The hay's already in. It's been a fantastic summer. The crop is looking really good. Why would I sell?'

'Can you afford the machines? Will you get it in before the rain?'

'Yes. It'll be tight, but we'll be fine. And once it's safe in the barn we'll be all set.' Farmer Wolstenholme smiled. 'It's like I've always said, Bartholomew, the farm's not for sale. However much money you offer me. This is our home. Annie's buried here, Isla and I live here, we always have. I'm sorry, but selling it is just not something I could ever do.'

Mr Busby shook his head. Suddenly the mood changed and his white teeth flashed, like a panther.

'I would strongly advise you to reconsider, Anthony. You never know what can happen.'

'What do you mean?'

Mr Busby leant forward. 'Well, let's be honest, you're not the luckiest man, are you?'

Farmer Wolstenholme looked puzzled. 'I'm sorry?'

'Wasn't this a pig farm before your father-in-law messed up?'

'Excuse me?'

'And then your wife died.'

'What's that got to do with anything?'

'Well, it's pretty unlucky. I mean, you got the insurance money, but I bet that's all gone. You must have borrowed more money to cover the harvest.'

Farmer Wolstenholme got up and went over to the sink. His hands were shaking and the glass rattled against the tap as he filled it with water. The other farmer cracked his knuckles and smiled. He got up, walked over and put his arm around Farmer Wolstenholme.

'I thought so,' continued Mr Busby. 'Listen, you'll probably be fine, but what would happen if there was a disaster? If it rained? Ruined the crops? Eh? That would be just your luck. To be left with nothing? Bankrupt? Homeless? I could make all that worry disappear. Isla would never have to worry again.'

At the mention of his daughter's name, Farmer Wolstenholme shrugged off the man's arm. 'No!'

The atmosphere changed again. Mr Busby walked to the door and then turned back. 'Don't be a fool, Anthony. You know you're unlucky. It's in your blood. You're going to lose everything. I'm offering you a fair price. Take it or leave it.'

'I think you should go now.' Farmer Wolstenholme looked determined.

'There's a storm coming, Anthony. I want this farm.'

'Get out!'

As Mr Busby left by the back door, Isla came into the kitchen looking very scared.

'Dad, what's happening? Why were you shouting?'

'Nothing, my love. Just Mr Busby getting the wrong end of the stick.'

'Is it true we're going bankrupt? Will we be homeless?'

Farmer Wolstenholme took a deep breath and knelt down so he was level with Isla.

'You know I've always been honest with you? That ever since Mum died I've always treated you as a grown-up?'

Isla nodded and tried her hardest to look grown-up.

'For a while, a few years ago, the farm was losing money. We've never had much money, but things were even worse. Grandpa wasn't a very good businessman, so we took over and things were a bit tough. Then we lost your mum and I had to do it on my own. And that was really difficult.'

'I sold those biscuits.'

Her dad smiled at her. 'I know you did, love, and it worked. We're fine. Once this crop of barley is in the barn, then I can sell it, pay off almost all our debts and we'll be good. Don't get me wrong, we won't be going on holiday to Disneyland – we probably won't have a holiday at all – but we'll be okay.'

Outside the house Rhona was hanging on every word, completely gripped. Heather, however, was bored. She yawned and looked longingly at the pear which, if anything, had got even juicier and heavier since she last looked. As she stared, a single drop of moisture slid slowly down the curvy side of the pear, hung for a second, suspended in the moonlight, and then dropped, glinting, to the ground below. Heather's parched mouth flooded with imagined pear juice and she shifted, hungrily. Then, almost as if that drop of moisture had finally tipped the scales, things started to happen. The pear finally snapped the stalk that held it in place, the branch whipped up with a liberated twang, and the whole tree seemed to straighten with relief. The pear hung motionless for a second before plummeting, silent as a bomb, down down down to the waiting cushion of grass below. For a split second Heather was frozen, then she whinnied with delight and, completely forgetting that Rhona was delicately balanced on her shoulders, leapt up and galloped towards the fallen treasure.

Inside the house Farmer Wolstenholme was just giving his daughter a very emotional hug when they both heard Heather's delighted whinny, and as they looked at the window they saw Rhona flying up into the air before dropping out of sight with a tragic *beeeeeh* followed by a loud thump. They raced over to the window and saw Rhona sprawled on the ground in a tangle of limbs, looking furiously at a completely oblivious and happily munching Heather.

It was three days after what Rhona was now crossly referring to as the 'eaves-dropping' incident and Heather and Isla were outside the ruined castle by the stream. This was where Isla's mum was buried and where Isla had her vegetable patch. The two of them often came here when they wanted to get away; they could skim stones and paddle and watch the occasional fish flicker past while Isla told her mum what was going on and tended the vegetables. Isla had uprooted a stalk of Brussels sprouts and was twisting the little buds off and putting them in a bag. Occasionally she'd come across one she didn't like the look of and chuck it over to where Heather was chewing contentedly. Isla had told her mum all about pet day and was now explaining about the school trip she'd just been on.

'. . . So anyway Miss Stephenson said we had to research facts about where we came from and she took us all into Alford to go to the library, and it was amazing because there were all these really old books and maps about what it was like here in the olden days, and actually the fields and stuff haven't hardly changed at all, but Alford's got so much bigger and before it was just like a village with a few huts, but then when they built the road it got much more important. But what I had to tell you was about the ghost who lives here. The librarian, when I told him where I lived, told me this really cool story. It's all about this man who was fighting against the English, and the English won so he ran away and hid, and then by accident his son told the troops where he was hiding, and so now the son's ghost is stuck here until he can make up for what he did. I mean, it wasn't his fault but that's the story and I wondered if you'd seen him, because you're like a ghost too. Kinda. I mean, you're not hundreds of years old, but you're still dead. Do ghosts get older? Do you always stay like you are when you die? The same clothes and everything? Imagine if you had your worst T-shirt on when you died. You'd be stuck in it for ever.'

'Hi love, I thought I'd find you here.'

Isla turned around to see her dad standing behind her. 'Hi Dad, I was just telling Mum about the history topic we're doing at school. It's about connecting yourself to the past and we have to find out stuff about where we live and so on. So I was telling Mum about how this place is haunted by a ghost who's been here for hundreds of years.'

Mr Wolstenholme took off his cap. He looked around him at the ruined castle with the stream babbling away as it raced past the cairn of stones where he'd buried Annie six years ago. He smiled ruefully as he remembered the moment when he and Isla had solemnly said a few words and prepared to scatter the ashes. First Isla couldn't get the lid off the urn and then he couldn't either. They'd wrestled with it, before both giving up and smiling sadly as Isla dug a hole with her bucket and spade and they'd buried the urn and then marked it with a pile of stones. That had been a day like today, crisp and sharp, the air sitting so light you could see all the way to Alford. Spongy, bouncy heather stretching away for ever, a purple carpet of blues and greens, damp with dew as it sparkled off into the distance.

He sat down next to his daughter, tickled Heather behind her ear and then picked up a stick and threw it. Heather looked at him in alarm; surely he didn't expect her to fetch it?

'Your grandad used to say that's why the tree doesn't flower.' He pointed at the tree which stood in the ruins of the castle, its branches bare and lifeless.

Isla stared at it. 'Isn't it dead?'

The farmer smiled. 'No, very much alive. It is a medlar tree. The fruit makes great jam, or it would if there ever was any. But until the ghost makes things better it will never flower or produce any fruit. Rubbish, of course, but that's the legend.'

'So it's like a ghost tree?'

Her dad laughed. 'I guess it is.'

'That's so cool! Wait till I tell Millie!'

'Come on. Let's go home. It's getting late and you're helping me harvest in the morning.'

As the three of them headed back to the farm with Isla chattering away, something made Heather look back towards the stream and the vegetable patch. The wind was blowing through the branches, making the tree wave to her – almost as if it was trying to get her attention, warning her about something. Heather shivered. She wasn't cold but there was a chill in the air. Almost like winter was coming or, at least, *something* was. It made her feel scared. Quickly she turned her back and scampered off after the other two.

Chapter 4

Spicy Pizza
& Boyfriends

The next morning everyone was up really early. Isla was off school because she had to help her dad. He had borrowed a combine harvester which was attached to the back of the tractor, and they drove to the field where he started harvesting the barley. Even though she'd done it a hundred times, Isla still loved riding in the tractor with her dad. There was just something so exciting about being really high up and watching him work all the really complicated knobs and levers that were needed to make the tractor go in a straight line.

It was still dark when they got to the field and they used the tractor headlights to eat the sausage sandwiches they'd made before they left. A couple of neighbours were helping out so everyone stood around and chatted, their breath visible in the cold pre-dawn air. Millie and another of Isla's schoolmates had come along as well, all glad of the chance to be off school and outside all day. Even though she was wearing her thickest fleece and the bobble hat her dad had given her for Christmas, it was still very cold and Isla was glad she was so excited or she would have been very shivery. Then, just as her dad was finishing his coffee, the sun started to inch over the horizon, and suddenly the field turned gold. Everybody leapt into action and, as they started their engines, Isla felt the sun glowing warm on her fleece, her heart racing as she squinted into the sun and watched the machines heading off into the midst of the bending, swaying barley.

Isla didn't stop all day. If she wasn't running to take a Thermos to her dad, she was making rolls and handing them out, or dashing around carrying petrol cans back and forth, running back to the house to get some wire and more tea and all the time the machines ploughed on, up and down the field, cutting huge paths through the barley and leaving nothing but flattened stalks behind them. It was as if someone had coloured in the field with a gold pencil and now a huge hand was taking a rubber and really neatly rubbing it out, one line at a time.

Heather, Rhona and Alastair turned up around lunchtime and Heather and Rhona settled down to watch while Alastair ran ahead of the machines, telling animals to get out of the way and trying to stop the younger rabbits playing dangerous games of chicken with the oncoming tractor. Heather was enjoying being with her friends on her own – Katy was right in the middle of hatching her eggs, so she had to stay where she was and it was quite nice to get away from her for a bit. She'd had the foresight to bring an apple with her

(*John Apple, soft, sweet and slightly chewy*), so she could practise two of her favourite things at the same time: doing nothing, and eating apples.

By the end of the day Isla was exhausted, and by the time they'd finished the harvest three days later, she was so stiff she felt as though Heather had been sitting on her. That night she and her dad got takeaway pizza and sat outside the barn eating it, almost too tired to talk. Heather was sitting next to Isla, longingly eyeing the little girl's pizza, although Isla seemed to be very hungry so she wasn't hopeful. Also, her friend had a habit of getting quite spicy pizza with funny green and red bits which made Heather's snout go a bit watery, so sharing with her was always risky.

'What happens next?' mumbled Isla to her dad.

'Don't talk with your mouth full. What do you mean?'

Isla swallowed. 'This is so good. The barley. What happens next? Will we sell it all?'

'It needs a week or so to dry out properly, inside the barn, and then, once that's done, I'll sell it.'

'And then everything will be okay? We won't be poor any more? We'll be able to buy things again? I don't know what, but the things we can't buy now.'

The farmer smiled at her and ruffled her hair. 'I'm afraid we'll always be poor, love. Farming's not something you do to make yourself rich. But once this lot is sold then the bank will stop sending me angry letters and maybe we can start thinking about getting you a new bike.'

'Yes! Can I get one like Millie's? She's got one with twenty-four gears so she can go up any hill she wants, and the tyres are really thick and chunky, which makes it really heavy to lift up, but she can ride over anything. It's called a trail bike because it can go on mountain trails and she says it's so cool, because she can just ride it anywhere, like in all the fields and even through the stream, and once she said she could drive it up the ramp in the skateboard park, but it's quite steep so she got stuck halfway up and she was trying and trying, but it was just too heavy so then she had to get Angus to pull it up for her, and she was so embarrassed because everyone says Angus has got a crush on Millie and really wants to be her boyfriend, but she really doesn't. Dad?'

'Mn-huh,' answered the farmer through a mouthful of pizza.

'Are we unlucky? I mean, always? Like that man who wanted to buy the farm said? About Mum?'

The farmer swallowed the last of his pizza, took a swig of his beer and put his arm slightly awkwardly around his daughter's shoulders.

'Your mum dying was the cruellest, most unfair thing that could ever have happened. My mother didn't die until I was about thirty and nor did your mum's mum.'

'Granny Helen?'

'Yes. She lived until she was seventy-seven, so you losing your mum when you weren't even four is really unfair and very unlucky.'

'What about the other stuff? The farm and Grandad and things? Are we unlucky about them as well?'

The farmer stretched out his hand and started ticking things off on his fingers. 'We live in the most beautiful place in the world, we've got loads of friends, we're both healthy, both full of pizza, we've harvested all the barley before the rain ruined it, and you won't have a boyfriend for about twenty more years—'

'Dad!' yelped an outraged Isla, punching him on the arm.

He smiled at her and punched her back. 'Do you remember her? Your mum, I mean.'

Isla looked thoughtful. 'Sometimes I think I can, but other times she's just kind of a person who's there but who doesn't really have a face or anything; she's just sort of there. I think she was smiley and I think she had curly hair? Kind of reddy-gold? But mostly I just imagine her and I go to the ruin and talk to her and tell her all about school and stuff and what me and Heather have been up to.'

She paused for a second.

'Do you think about Mum all the time? I mean, I do sometimes, but usually only when we're at the ruin. But you knew her for ages and you were always with her so it must be weirder for you. Are you finished? Can I have your crusts for Heather? Only she doesn't like mine because the chillies make them too spicy for her.'

Farmer Wolstenholme handed over his pizza box and watched as his daughter fed bits of pizza crust to the pig lying by her side.

'When your mother and I got engaged we had no money to buy a ring and I promised her one day I would buy her a proper ring with a proper precious stone and everything. The day you were born your mum told me this story. It's about a really rich woman who lived all alone in a huge, big house and she had loads of jewels, and every day she'd get them out and count them and be boasty about how rich she was with all her money and jewels. She never got married because she didn't want to share her money with anyone else.'

Isla grinned. 'Like a dragon. Guarding his treasure.'

'So one day, a poor washerwoman was lost in the forest and knocked at her door, and the rich woman let her in and took the poor woman to her treasure chamber and showed the woman all her jewels piled up in mountains. "Look at how rich I am," she said.

"Look at all my jewels. I am the luckiest woman in the world. How many jewels do *you* have? I'm sure you can't have as many as me!"

'That afternoon, the washerwoman got back to the tiny little hut where she lived by the side of the river, and as she drew closer four children came running out of the house.

' "Amber, Coral, Pearl, Ruby, come here and give me a hug," said the washerwoman happily, and as her children came running she knew she was the luckiest woman in the world.'

Isla made a face at him. 'That is the soppiest story you've ever told me. Ever.'

Isla's dad looked a bit upset. 'But the children were her jewels. Your mother didn't need a ring because—'

'Because I was her jewel. Like the washerwoman's kids. I get it, Dad,' interrupted Isla. 'It's a dad story. Lovely, but really soppy.'

And then, with no warning and a terrifying crack, lightning tore the sky apart and the rain started to fall. Isla, Heather and Farmer Wolstenholme ran and sheltered inside the barn.

'We're going to get wet,' said the farmer, grinning as he looked across the wet yard towards the farmhouse. Heather was sadly eyeing a pizza crust that had got abandoned in the rush and was getting soggier and soggier as it lay on the ground.

'Come on, Dad, let's make a break for it. See you tomorrow, Heather Duroc.' Isla gave Heather a last stroke, put one of the pizza boxes over her head as an umbrella and ran across the yard through the pounding rain.

Above their heads the heavens raged and roared – black clouds rolling, lightning crashing through the sky – almost as if darkness was closing in on the world, and the sun would never shine again.

Chapter 5

Leaking Roofs
& Ducks' Feet

The barn had been built about three hundred years before and was originally meant to store hay and horses. The walls were made of thick stone and half of the inside was divided into wooden stalls, usually empty, but now, following the harvest, crammed full of hay and barley. The animals slept where they wanted, normally snuggled up wherever they could get most comfy, although both Heather and Rhona had their own favourite stalls. Rhona's was full of old newspapers and magazines and Heather's was by the front door because that meant she could be sure she was first at the trough for mealtimes.

At one end of the barn was a sort of hayloft which you reached by climbing up a ladder. Apart from Heather and Rhona, the barn was home to some field mice, a couple of ferrets, an occasional owl and anyone else who happened to be around. Alastair was supposed to sleep in his kennel by the house, but quite often he got bored and came to the barn for a sleepover. Isla's chickens always slept in a coop by the farmhouse, although they usually had their supper with the others before going back there at bedtime. There was also a huge cellar underneath the barn, but it never got used, and as it was accessed through a trap door, it was very hard for the animals to get into.

So at the moment it was just the regular inhabitants of the barn and Alastair who were in the doorway watching the amazing storm rage outside. The rain was falling in almost solid sheets, drumming on the roof of the barn and smashing onto the yard outside, bouncing up and turning everything into a sea of mud. The sky was a dark purple colour as the branches and forks of lightning crashed through it and the thunder rolled and roared. Although Rhona kept telling them it was completely natural, Heather and the field mice were terrified by the noise and the lightning, raging like a dragon woken from his sleep.

'We've never had a storm like this before. What if we drown?' said Heather with a gulp.

Alastair was rather enjoying it. 'We won't drown, it's fine, we're safe in here.' He kept pretending the rain was like a sprinkler so he'd run outside, get really wet and then race back in again before madly shaking and drenching everyone else.

They watched the storm for a bit longer and then decided it was time to get to bed. Alastair said his kennel had a rather annoying leak, which dripped on him when it rained, so he'd be better off staying in the barn.

By the time the animals went to sleep, it was really late and they were all exhausted, which is why, an hour or so later, when a bolt of lightning hit the barn full on and sent sparks into the hay, nobody heard it and they all slept on.

Within minutes the hay had caught fire and was smoking; the flames started to catch and move rapidly through the barn as more and more of the hay and barley caught and started to burn. Thick black smoke began to fill the barn and that was what finally woke up a groggy Alastair. He looked sleepily at the flames and then sat bolt upright.

'Heather! Rhona! Wake up, we're on fire!'

Heather was by the door so she was fine, but Rhona's stall was at the back of the barn underneath the hayloft and the smoke was quite thick over there. Alastair raced over and barked at Rhona, but she was half asleep and half full of smoke so she didn't really register. He nudged her but it did no good, so he took a deep breath, said 'Sorry' as politely as he could, and gave her a good bite on the bottom.

'Owwww!' howled Rhona as she woke up and instinctively kicked out at Alastair with a hard hoof. He knew it was coming though and ducked, and then

Rhona saw what was happening and the two of them ran out of the barn to where Heather was waiting in the rain. The animals had practised fire drills, so normally they knew what to do, but because it was the middle of the night they'd all forgotten their jobs, so Rhona ran through them.

'Alastair, get over to the house and bark until Farmer Wolstenholme wakes up. Heather, go and make sure all the field mice are gone. They usually sleep at the back of your stall so I'm sure they're fine, but let's double-check. The ferrets and the barn owl weren't around tonight so that's everyone. I'm going to go and tell the chickens what's happening and I'll see you back here in two minutes.'

They all dashed off to do their jobs and soon the farmyard was filled with the sound of frenzied barking and clucking as Alastair tried to wake the humans, and the chickens demanded to know what was going on.

The mice were all gone from Heather's stall so when the three of them reassembled, everything seemed fine. By now the barn was visibly burning and they could feel the heat coming off it as they stood and watched. The rain had turned to drizzle, which didn't help as it meant there was nothing much to dampen the blaze. Lights came on in the farmhouse and soon the farmer and Isla both came out in dressing gowns and wellies to see what was going on. Heather snouted Isla as if to say, 'I'm fine', but then her dad grabbed the little girl and sent her back inside saying he was going to call the fire brigade and she must stay out of the way.

Suddenly Heather's heart stopped. 'Where's Katy?' she asked.

The animals all looked at each other.

'She's still inside. Her nest is in the hayloft,' said Rhona.

Alastair shook his head. 'She can't be! She'd have felt the heat of the fire.'

Rhona looked worried. 'Ducks don't have any nerves in their feet! She won't feel a thing.'

Alastair didn't waste any more time. He ran straight into the burning barn and all the way to the far end. The fire was everywhere now – it was hot under his paws, the flames licking up the walls of the barn. He got to the ladder leading up to the hay loft and shouted up.

'Katy! Are you up there? The barn's on fire! Come out!'

The terrified duck's head appeared in the doorway. 'I can't!'

Alastair couldn't stand now because the ground was getting so hot. 'You've got to! Fly down! Come on!'

'My eggs! They're hatching! I can't leave my chicks!'

'Wait here, I'll get the others.' Alastair ran and found Heather and Rhona. 'What can we do? We can't get up the ladder and her chicks can't fly, so she can't get out. She's completely trapped.'

There was a loud bang from the barn. The heat forced a bit of the roof to fly off as the wall started to crumble.

'We can't just leave her, she'll die!' cried Heather.

Rhona was thinking hard. 'There's the window round the back! Come on.' She ran off and the others followed.

The barn was built on two levels and there was a tool

shed outside with a roof the same height as the hayloft. In the old days there had been a door at the top to get hay in and out and at some point that door had been turned into a window. The animals jumped onto some logs, and from there onto the roof of the tool shed so they could peer through the window into the barn. The fire hadn't reached the tool shed yet, but it was surely only a matter of time, and as they looked they saw Katy frantically flapping her wings over her nest to try and keep the smoke and flames away from her chicks.

They knocked on the window and she looked at them in panic. She clearly wasn't going to abandon her chicks.

'We've got to break the window. Heather, can you do it?'

Heather flung herself at the window. Nothing. She ran and leapt again as hard as she could. The glass shook but stayed firm. She ran back, stared at the window with real anger and charged like she'd never charged before.

She hit the window with a massive thump and a big crack appeared right down the middle of the glass.

The crack weakened the window and the pressure from the fire inside blasted it out, showering the three animals with glass and letting air rush into the burning barn.

'Come on!' cried Rhona.

The three friends leapt through the window into the hayloft. They were forced back by the heat and the flames, but they struggled onwards and panted their way to Katy who was gasping for air as she desperately sheltered her nest from the burning ashes that were flying around inside the building.

There were five chicks in the nest, newborn and helpless, and all cheeping frantically. More floorboards collapsed as the flames licked up.

'We've got to get you out!' said Rhona, shouting to make herself heard above the fire.

'I'm not leaving them!' shouted Katy.

'Then we'll take all of you!' said Rhona. 'Can they walk?'

Katy shook her head. 'Don't be stupid! They're terrified!'

The nest was snug in the corner of the barn.

Rhona and Alastair pulled at it but they couldn't move it. A bit of the floor under Heather collapsed and she jumped to one side. 'Rhona! Do something!'

The goat leant into the nest, picked up one of the chicks in her mouth, and ran out through the window. The others copied her. Four chicks were safe.

'There's one more!' said Katy. 'I'm going back!' She turned to the window, but there was a whoosh and flames shot up between them and the nest. It was a wall of fire. There was no way through!

Katy was sobbing as sirens drew nearer, but they wouldn't arrive in time for the last chick. Suddenly Alastair leapt through the window into the flames. Heather and Rhona ran forward, but there was thick smoke billowing, blocking everything.

For a second the smoke cleared and they saw inside. Most of the floor had gone and Alastair was carefully inching along a beam towards the nest. The animals held their breath, but then, just as he reached it, there was a massive bang, the flames shot up, the blast flung the animals back, and the beam, Alastair and the nest disappeared in a ball of flame.

Rhona and Heather picked themselves up and ran around to the front of the barn as the sound of sirens came up the road, closely followed by two fire engines arriving in the farmyard.

Within minutes the firefighters had run their hoses to the stream, targeted them on the barn and were pouring water into the inferno, struggling to control the flames as they licked into the sky and devoured the building.

In complete despair the two friends sat silently side by side, both lost in their own thoughts as they watched it burn, still hoping for a miracle, but each fearing deep down that they'd seen the last of their friend. Heather's eyes were watering – she wasn't sure whether it was tears or the sheer force of the heat from the fire – when suddenly her heart leapt as a blackened, smoking figure burst out of the flaming doorway, landed on his feet and then collapsed on the ground in front of them. His coat was smoking, he was soaked and blackened, his eyes were bloodshot and his chest was heaving, but as he lay half dead on the ground, he opened his mouth and a beautiful, clean, fluffy, yellow chick emerged. It shook itself dry, looked at the sheepdog and cheeped crossly, before pottering off to find its mother.

Heather galloped over to Alastair and licked his face as he panted and gasped, while Rhona fetched the farmer, who gently picked up the dog and carried him into the farmhouse.

For the rest of the night Rhona and Heather slept in the chicken coop and then the next day they went out to survey the damage. The barn was destroyed, the roof was completely gone, most of the walls as well, and although the tool shed seemed to have survived pretty much unharmed, it didn't look good. Alastair was still a bit coughy and wheezy. Isla and her dad had washed him down and cut away the scorched fur, and the vet had said he was going to be fine.

Despite all this, Heather was quite chirpy. Nobody had died, after all. In fact, as she munched on an apple she'd found in the field (*Peck's Pleasant, highly aromatic, green-coloured becoming bright yellow with orange-red blush*), she was humming to herself, until

Rhona pointed to where Farmer Wolstenholme was standing with Isla, gazing sadly at his ruined barn. What little of the crops hadn't burnt in the fire had then been destroyed by the firefighters' water, and the farmer was contemplating the wreckage of his business. His hopes and dreams had quite literally gone up in smoke. Rhona mouthed to Heather to *shh* and listen.

'We weren't covered against fire. Everything else, but not fire. It's Scotland, it doesn't burn here, it rains. So unlucky. It could have sleeted, snowed, blown a tornado even, that would all have been fine. Just not fire.'

Heather whispered to Rhona, 'What does he mean "not covered"? What about the roof?'

'He means insurance cover. When humans think something might go wrong or they might lose something, they pay a bit of money to someone in case it does. Then if they lose the thing, or there's a disaster, the person they've paid gives them back the value of the thing they've lost. It's a bit like when squirrels save loads of nuts. Even if they can't find any food in the winter, they know they won't starve because they've got the saved nuts. It's called insurance.'

Heather sighed. 'I've tried doing that saving food thing, but it's so hard. I did it with some apples and then forgot where I'd put them. I was in a real panic and then Alastair remembered where they were. So lucky I'd told him.'

'There you go. You thought you might forget so you told Alastair. That's insurance.' The goat smiled at Heather, who didn't look any wiser.

'But what if I hadn't? Just imagine if they'd been lost for ever? It would be like not eating something twice!' She shuddered at the memory. 'So is it bad then, this insurance thing?'

Rhona looked very gloomy. 'I rather fear it is, yes.'

And as usual, Rhona was absolutely right. With his crops ruined and no insurance, Farmer Wolstenholme couldn't repay any of his debts and certainly couldn't afford to start again. He was left with no choice but to sell the farm to Mr Busby, and at a considerably lower price than the chicken farmer had been offering him before.

Mr Busby wanted to move in immediately, so within a little over two weeks Isla had to leave the place where she'd been so happy and prepare for life in London, staying with her Uncle Max until they could find a flat of their own. Saying goodbye to her mum and her friends at school was one of the hardest things Isla had ever had to do.

But that was nothing compared to how she felt about having to break the news to Heather . . .

Chapter 6

The
Wildcat Flap

Heather was worried. Something was up with Isla and she didn't know what it was. Isla hadn't told her. It had been ages since the little girl had last brought out her slops, or smuggled her some carrots or come for a sleepover in the barn. Not that she could do that any more as the animals were sleeping in the tool shed. Actually, it was fine and quite roomy, but there wasn't any straw so Isla wouldn't have been very comfy. Heather went and found Rhona, who was eating her way through a newspaper and clearly was not keen on being disturbed.

'Isla's not talking to me.'

Rhona ignored her.

Heather waited patiently for about two seconds. 'She's ignoring me. What's wrong?'

Rhona sighed and looked up from chewing her paper. 'How long has she not been talking to you? Only last time you got all hot and bothered it was about one hour and that was because of pet day, so forgive me if I don't seem very worried.' She crossly went back to her newspaper.

Heather thought for a minute.

'Since the night of the fire. She came out in her dressing gown and gave me a big hug and then she had to go inside again. That was the last time. Since then, nothing.'

Rhona looked up again. 'Oh dear.'

'What?' said Heather in a panic. 'What's "Oh dear"? What does that mean?'

'I think she's had some bad news. Sounds to me—'

'But that doesn't make sense!' interrupted Heather. 'She always tells me bad news. She says I make it easier because she can just talk and I don't interrupt.'

'Lucky girl,' said Rhona pointedly.

'So what can it be? And why hasn't she told me? She tells me everything!' Heather was turning on the spot frantically.

'I rather fear the news may be about you. That is, about all of us. I suspect that, because of the damage to the crops and not being insured, Farmer Wolstenholme has had to sell the farm to that sinister man named after a hat. If they were moving to another farm Isla would be taking you with her, so the fact that she isn't telling you to pack your bags points to something rather different.'

Heather didn't understand much of that. 'Moving? Where?'

Rhona went back to her newspaper. 'Why don't you go and ask her? Or at least let her know you're worried. That you've noticed that she isn't talking to you.'

But Heather was already gone.

Isla was sitting on her bed, absolutely miserable. For once in her life she was completely lost for words. How was she going to tell Heather they were moving to London? She'd been trying to get it straight in her head for days, but how do you explain to someone that you're going away from her, but not because of her? And you're not taking her with you, not because you don't love her but because you can't! It was hard enough understanding it herself, let alone trying to explain it to someone else. And the worst of it was that the one person she wanted to talk to about it was the one person she couldn't! Why couldn't there be two Heathers? Then she could talk to one about how to talk to the other or something like that.

As she was desperately trying to think of how to explain the inexplicable, she heard something. She got up, put on her slippers and went to investigate. There were very strange sounds coming from inside the kitchen – sort of scrabbling noises, a bit like someone trying to get in. She picked up her rounders bat, and tiptoed into the kitchen.

Isla burst out laughing at the sight that confronted her. There was an old, disused cat flap in the kitchen door, and Heather's head and one of her front legs were stuck through it as she tried the impossible task of getting the rest of her rather large body through a hole designed for a skinny cat. She was straining and huffing and puffing and Isla suspected she might actually have realised her mistake and was now trying to go backwards, but couldn't manage that either. Heather's eyes were wide open and she looked so scared and upset that Isla's heart melted and she raced over to her friend and gave her head the biggest hug she'd ever given her. And as she looked at her big ears flopping over her troubled, deep, brown eyes, Isla's floodgates opened and the words came pouring out.

'I'm so glad you're here, I've been missing you so much and I've been so desperate to talk to you, but I didn't know how to say what I've got to say and that's that we're moving to London next week because of the fire, and I can't take you with me, and it's making me really sad, and I don't know what the answer is and I don't want to leave you or the farm and I'm really scared of going to London, and I think Dad is too, but he's being really brave because we have to go and Mr Busby has promised that you and Rhona can stay here, and he even said that we could come back and visit you, so maybe we'll do that, but I just didn't know how to tell you that I was going, and then I felt awful but I wanted to get what I had to say to you just right before I said it, but that's really silly because we always understand each other anyway whatever happens, don't we?'

With a superhuman effort Heather pushed her head further inside the cat flap and gave Isla her very best headbutt, and so, when Farmer Wolstenholme came home, he was met by a pig's bottom that was sticking out of his kitchen door and yet somehow radiated extreme happiness.

Two weeks later, Farmer Wolstenholme moved out and Farmer Busby moved in. Heather would never forget that day, not least because only twenty-four hours before, they'd had a very unwelcome visitor.

Heather had been carefully listing all the different varieties of apple she knew (*Cox, Howgate Wonder, Magnum Gala, Grenadier, Scotch Bridget* and so on), when suddenly, out of the hen coop slipped the long, sleek body of the wildcat. He was over a metre long from nose to tail, his fur was striped black and brown like the bark of a tree, and he moved in total silence. Lately he'd been stealing chickens more and more, but he'd never come in daylight before and seeing him there, all teeth and smoking eyes, was terrifying. He extended his razor sharp claws and yawned.

There was a deathly hush, everybody stood stock still and then he spoke.

'Hello everyone. How nice to see you all. It's like a sort of living picnic.'

The animals all seemed to be hiding behind Heather, so very shakily she spoke up. 'What do you want?'

The wildcat yawned again, the muscles rippling

under his skin. 'Good question. Should it be pig? Perhaps duck? Maybe even goat? No, on second thoughts, I want a chicken. Where are the chickens?'

Heather gulped. She knew that the chickens and Katy's ducklings had gone to have a little splash in the stream at the bottom of the garden, but that was a while ago. They'd be coming back soon, probably any minute, in fact.

'They're not here. Why don't you have something else? Like a nice . . . c-carrot?' she stammered.

The wildcat looked at her in disbelief. 'A carrot! Do you have any idea what I am?'

Heather swallowed. 'C-c-cat?'

The wildcat looked at her in amused disbelief.

'*Wild*cat. Britain's only remaining large, wild predator. I am a carnivore. I eat meat. Just meat. I get all my nutrition from meat. Because of that, my body is uniquely designed to hunt animals, catch them, kill them and eat them. If I were hunting you, my canine teeth would kill you by severing your spinal cord. Then my back teeth would act like scissors and shear through your flesh, making it easy and quick to digest. So no, kind though the offer is, I do not want a carrot!'

Heather gulped nervously. 'Or lettuce, maybe?'

There was a sudden blur of movement and the next thing Heather knew she was on her back with claws digging into her throat and the wildcat's muzzle in her ear. 'The chickens aren't in the coop, Fatty, so where are they?'

Heather had never been more scared in her life. Frantically she started gabbling. 'They're not here. Eggs! Weak eggs! Farmer! Vet! He's the vet, and chickens. All of them. I can hear his car!'

'Liar!' The wildcat sunk his claws a little deeper into Heather's neck. 'The only reason you're not already dead is that you're too fat to carry back to my wife and children.'

Heather tried to stay calm and then her heart sank. Round the corner of the house she caught sight of a little troop of slightly damp chickens, all happily walking back towards the farmyard, heads bobbing as they came. They hadn't seen the wildcat yet and nor had he seen them, but it was only a matter of seconds unless she could do something.

Thinking fast, Heather said in as wavery a voice as possible, 'Please don't eat me. I've got an ill piglet in the barn. He'll die if I'm not there to look after him.'

As she spoke she looked over at Rhona and nodded her head towards the house. Fortunately the wildcat was distracted at the thought of such easy prey.

'A sick piglet, eh? What a caring mother you are. Bit stupid, though. Get out of my way.'

He released Heather and padded towards the barn while Rhona discreetly sidled over to head off the chickens and lead them to safety.

Then disaster struck. Out of the ruins of the barn sauntered the now almost fully recovered Alastair who, on finding himself face to face with the wildcat, was momentarily stunned and then charged, barking like crazy. The wildcat turned tail and raced back across the farmyard, straight at the row of chickens. All hell broke loose as the wildcat tore into the chickens and, when the feathers settled and the dust cleared, the wildcat was gone, but so was one of the chickens. The animals were devastated; only Rhona was calm.

'It's a bad omen,' she said gloomily. 'Everything is changing.'

And then the very next day, Farmer Wolstenholme loaded up the car and walked around his farm for the last time.

Heather knew it was leaving day and she was having a root in the yard behind the barn, trying not to think about it, when Isla found her and threw her arms round her neck.

'I've tried really hard to be brave and not say goodbye so I wouldn't cry, but I just thought I've got to not be silly, and don't interrupt me because it'll make me cry, but I know I'm going to see you again, so this is just half goodbye because we'll see each other really soon, and I don't know when, but we definitely will because we're best friends and best friends always see each other, and that's why the French call it *au revoir* which means something like "until the seeing again" or something, and I'm going to give you the coin you found because then I know

I'll see you again really soon, because you've got to give it back, so make sure you look after it because I want it back when I see you next time. Scrunch if that's a plan.'

She unwrapped herself from around Heather's neck and looked at her. Heather blinked a couple of times and then scrunched her snout as hard as she could. Then she leant in and butted Isla, her rough skin stroking the little girl's cheek. Isla could feel things bubbling up inside her and didn't want to speak, so she took the coin on its bit of string from around her neck and put it around Heather's.

'Isla, come on, love!' came her dad's voice from around the corner and Isla got up and stroked Heather's snout one final time. Then she turned and ran.

'See you later, Heather Duroc!' shouted the little girl in a wobbly voice over her shoulder as she disappeared around the barn. Heather couldn't move, and by the time she'd unfrozen and galloped around the corner, the farmer's car was disappearing out of the farmyard, taking her best friend with it.

All the next week Heather was in a really bad mood, snapping at everyone, not eating properly and then being all fidgety and restless. The others were getting sick of it and finally Rhona lost her temper.

'Will you stop it? Why don't you do something instead of just grumping around?'

Heather sighed. 'There's nothing to do. I'm bored.'

'For heaven's sake, you've got a whole farmyard to play in. Go and root by the river or something. Or there are all these new chickens. Talk to them. Help them settle in.'

It was true that now that Mr Busby was in charge there were Leghorns, Light Sussex and Scots Dumpy chickens all running about all over the place and making a real racket from morning till night. The big barn had been swiftly rebuilt as the processing plant for the chickens. According to Rhona, who had stood on a box on another box to peer in, it was all conveyor belts and machinery for putting bits of chicken into packets and stuff. First thing in the morning, once a week, the lorries would arrive and be loaded up with packets of Busby's free-range organic chicken thighs, or breasts, or drumsticks. It made them all shiver a bit, knowing the chickens would go into the barn squawking and clucking and come out on a plastic tray. The chickens didn't seem to mind though, and they had a happy time scratching about in the yard and fields before they disappeared.

'You need to take your mind off Isla. Why don't you go for a run?' suggested Alastair one morning.

Heather looked at him in horror. A run? Her? But he was right about one thing, she did need to distract herself. She got up and went in search of Rhona.

'Alastair reckons I should do something to take my mind off Isla.'

'He's bright, that boy,' said Rhona approvingly. 'You going to go for a run?'

'What is it with you two and running? No, I want you to teach me to read.'

Chapter 7

Bin Bags
& Fish and Chips

Rhona had been reading for as long as she could remember. Right from the moment she'd first munched her way through a catalogue of tractor parts she'd basically devoured anything she could find. Magazines about fishing, letters, farming information and other stuff. Even some pink magazines about princesses that Isla had given her.

These days, though, Rhona's reading material came from Mr Busby's rubbish bin, so it was mostly cereal boxes and plastic bags. That was fine, but it did mean a lot of weird words like Weetabix and Costcutter, Kwik Save and Cheerios.

Once Rhona had explained that Heather didn't *have* to eat the words to read them, they got started. They began with the alphabet – *A* is for apple, *B* for barn, *C* for cornflakes, and so on. Once she'd given her the basics, Rhona moved on to getting Heather to sound out the letters and trying to work out the words with the help of pictures.

As the lessons went on, Rhona assured her she was making steady progress, although Heather secretly told Alastair she wasn't any good at reading and was only really carrying on because Rhona seemed to be enjoying it so much. As far as she could tell, reading wasn't something Duroc pigs were really cut out for. And it wasn't stopping her thinking about Isla. Coco Pops just reminded her of her friend's eyes. In fact, one morning Heather was feeling so much like not having a lesson that when she heard Rhona calling her she scampered behind the farmhouse and hid until her friend's voice had faded into the distance – and the lesson with it.

As she heaved a sigh of relief she looked around her and realised that actually she was in rather an interesting spot, which was home to a rather interesting smell. It seemed to be coming from the large black bag that had been left by the bin. Thoughtfully she sat on her haunches, pointed her snout skywards and filled her nose with the smell. Definitely potato skins, old fish bones, something spicy, and milk that had gone off. But there was something else she couldn't place. Something intriguing. What was it? Furtively she looked around and, seeing no one, she gripped the bag in her teeth, swung it in the air and gave it a few good kicks with her trotter until, like a birthday piñata, it split open and poured its contents onto the ground.

Heather couldn't believe her eyes. For a good five minutes she just sat on her haunches and gazed at the paradise before her. There were potato peelings, banana skins, Brussels sprouts, bits of cheese, an apple core (*Scotch Dumpling, a cooking apple which cooks to a frothy purée with a good flavour*), milk cartons, even an old corn cob. That was the mystery smell: corn cob. She felt like the luckiest pig in the whole world. A tear of happiness rolled down her cheek, and then, as she was swallowing the saliva that was threatening to flood her mouth, she saw it. Right at the bottom of the bag and only just visible, poking out from underneath a piece of paper, was her third favourite food in the whole world: a glistening, crunchy, delectable, orange carrot. Heather swallowed, and ever so gently she fixed her eyes on the carrot, nudged the bag over onto its side, lifted the bit of paper that said *Heather Duroc* off the top of it, lowered her snout and inhaled deeply. The smell was heavenly, a little bit too ripe, slightly sweet but—

Hang on. She stopped and thought about what she'd just seen: *the piece of paper that said Heather Duroc*. She looked again and sure enough, there it was, in blue pen on the piece of paper, the words *Heather Duroc*. There was other writing but she couldn't read the rest. She looked again and sounded it out. It was definitely her name. Then it struck her:

she'd read her own name. Without thinking about it, or worrying which letter was which, or whether it was a doing word or not, she'd read her own name! Rhona would be so pleased with her. She was so pleased with herself. She could read. But while she was still glowing with pride and picturing how she was going to tell Rhona, something else occurred to her. What was her name doing on a piece of paper? And why was it in the rubbish bin?

Heather sat down. Suddenly her head felt very crowded with stuff, and it muddled her. There were too many things to think about and she didn't know where to start. She'd never been on a piece of paper before. Humans were on pieces of paper. Not pigs. Unless they were going to be . . . sold. She squealed and jumped up. Frantically, she started turning round and round on the spot. She was going to be sold! When? Where would she go? It must be like when Farmer Wolstenholme had got her certificated. She'd heard him explaining to Isla that he was having to get a certificate to prove she was an organically reared, pure-breed Duroc so he could mate her with other pigs. But if it was a certificate, then why was it in the rubbish? Maybe she wasn't an organically reared, pure-breed Duroc? Maybe it said she was just a fat old sow. If she wasn't a Duroc any more, then she'd definitely be sold. Or eaten. Or sold *and* eaten! Heather collapsed on her belly and her eyes filled with tears. If only she hadn't read the bit of paper. Now she was going to be sold and she didn't even know when. Today might be her last day. If only Rhona hadn't made her read and forced her to hide by the rubbish. It was all Rhona's fault!

That thought made her cross. Rhona had signed her death warrant. She wasn't quite sure what that meant, but her friend had said it about the wildcat after one of his particularly vicious raids and it sounded very important. She'd better go and find her immediately. She picked up the bit of paper and got another waft of carrot smell. Her tummy rumbled. She realised that it had been rumbling for the last five minutes but she'd been so muddled she hadn't noticed. She looked at all the food spilling out of the bag and the carrot, still glistening where it lay, tempting her, calling to her. She looked around. There was nobody about. Perhaps just a quick snack to keep her going, and then she'd go and get her friend. After all, she'd just had a nasty shock; she needed to keep her strength up. Very carefully she put the piece of paper to one side, surveyed the ocean of delicacies around the plastic bag and licked her chops.

'It's a letter,' said Rhona when Heather showed it to her. 'It's addressed to you, here at the farm.'

Heather was pleased and cross all at once. 'Who's sent me a letter? And why wasn't it delivered to me?'

Rhona looked puzzled. 'Perhaps Mr Busby doesn't know who Heather Duroc is. Where did you find it anyway?'

Heather was suddenly strangely embarrassed as she pictured herself rooting through the rubbish. 'Oh, nowhere special. You know. Can't really remember. Just around. Here and there.'

Rhona raised an eyebrow and looked at her

friend curiously. 'You've got chocolate on your snout, by the way.'

Heather blushed but luckily, being red already, it didn't show.

She nosed the piece of paper and asked in a quick sort of voice, 'What does it say?'

Rhona shrugged. 'I don't know. It's just the envelope. When people send letters they put them inside an envelope which is addressed to whoever they want to receive it. Then the postman knows where to deliver it. This one's got your name written and then our address underneath. But it's been opened. The letter has been taken out.'

'But it was my letter!' said Heather crossly, forgetting her embarrassment for a minute. 'Where is it? It was addressed to me.'

Rhona nodded. 'Yes, and perhaps whoever opened it threw it away when they realised it wasn't for them. The letter was probably with the envelope. Shame you can't remember where you found it or we could have gone and looked.' Rhona raised an eyebrow at her friend for the second time that morning. 'Hmm?'

Heather sighed. 'Okay, but I'm only taking you.'

Heather led the way towards the back of the house where she'd found the letter. As they rounded the corner Rhona's eyes nearly popped out of her head. It was carnage; there was rubbish everywhere. Yogurt pots, newspapers, takeaway boxes, bills, bits of an old dishcloth, leaflets, cigarette packets, milk cartons – all sorts. They were scattered all over the place, and all spotless. It was as though each object had been picked up, examined and then licked clean, which, in a way, it had. Rhona turned to look at her friend, and this time both eyebrows went skywards.

Heather had the grace to look rather sheepish and she pawed at the ground distractedly. 'I was really hungry. But it was mostly paper. There wasn't much actual food. Not really.'

Rhona couldn't help but smile at her friend.

'Well, there certainly isn't any left now, is there? Now, shall we try and find this letter?'

Dear Auntie Heather,

Our project for this term is 'connecting ourselves to the world' and we have to write a letter to someone, so I picked you.

My new school is called St Anthony's and it's a bit weird, although my teacher Miss Grey is really nice. It's got this brown uniform, so Miss Grey says when we stand in a line we look like a box of chocolate fingers, and it's in this place called Elephant and Castle, which sounds cool, but there's no elephants or castles anywhere and every time I read the sign it just reminds me about home, only this castle isn't ruined.

The food at school is funny. Lamb stew and things. Friday is good because it's fish and chips. Miss Grey says all schools have fish and chips on Fridays. Do you think that means the fish swim extra fast on Thursday so they don't get caught?

It's probably best that you didn't come to London with me. I don't think you'd like it here. There's a garden outside my bedroom, but it's for everyone in the building and there's only a teeny bit of grass so you couldn't really root properly.

Love Isla

xoxoxoxoxoxoxox

PS - This is me in my uniform.

It was well past the animals' bedtime, but nobody was asleep. Everyone had assembled to inspect the letter. It was dark so they were clustered around the security light by the barn. As it was turned on and off by movement, it kept going out so Alastair had to keep running under it every minute or so to set it off again. It was the first time any of them had ever got a letter, and they were all thrilled. All except Heather. She was worriedly munching an apple (*McIntosh, a crisp red apple with bright white flesh and a refreshing, sweet flavour*) and frowning at the picture Isla had drawn of herself. 'Read it again.'

So Rhona started to read it again. '*Dear Auntie Heather—*'

'Stop. Something's not right. I mean, why is she writing to me? And why is she calling me Auntie Heather?'

'She's missing you?' suggested Alastair tentatively.

'But I'm a pig! There's no point sending me a letter. I'm not that good at reading. And even if I was, how would she know that?'

Rhona raised an eyebrow. 'She's Isla. When did she

ever do things that made sense? Perhaps she thought Mr Busby would read it to you.'

Heather snorted dismissively. 'As if! I doubt he even knows I'm a pure-breed organically reared Duroc. Isla would know he'd chuck it straight in the bin.'

She flopped down exhausted with all that thinking and looked around her at the puzzled faces. Alastair raised a paw questioningly.

'Maybe she doesn't expect you to answer. Maybe she's just missing you. When she talks to you, she just talks and talks and talks because you can't answer her. That's what the letter's like. She's just being Isla-ish.'

Heather nodded. 'Go on.'

'She's never been able to keep things from you. She always tells you everything, so that's what she's doing. She can't tell her dad she hates London and is miserable because then he'd feel guilty, but she had to tell someone. Like when I bit that sheep and I tried to keep it secret, but in the end I couldn't. I had to own up.'

'Has Isla bitten a sheep?' asked one of Katy's ducklings.

Heather shook her head. 'No. Alastair's right. She's

talking to me as if I was in the room with her. It's like she's asking for help.' Her ears flopped down over her eyes and she looked miserable. Then she flicked them back, raised her snout and cleared her throat. 'If Isla wants to be here but can't be here, then here's got to be where she is – that is, there.'

Everyone looked a bit blank.

'I'm going to London.'

'What?! But London's like a million miles away. It's in England. Right at the bottom of England. How are you going to get there?' asked Rhona.

Heather looked daunted, but at the same time utterly determined.

'I have absolutely no idea.'

Chapter 8

Lights, Camera, Pig!

But the next day something happened which changed everything. When everyone woke up, the farm was unrecognisable. There were strangers doing things all over the place, new vans full of equipment, and somebody was hosing down the yard until it gleamed like never before. Once it was spotless, six bales of straw were positioned like a grand chair in the middle of the yard, and huge lights lit it up like a straw throne.

Rhona was standing watching it all when Heather sidled over to her.

'What's going on?' asked Heather, trying to keep the excitement out of her voice.

'They're building a set. Must be about to take photos.'

'Of the straw?'

'Of course not. Someone will sit on the straw bales and those big lights will shine at them.'

Sure enough, shortly afterwards Mr Busby emerged from the farmhouse in a very smart pair of brand new blue overalls and a blue cap with a black peak. He was accompanied by a tall, skinny man with blond hair, very tight jeans and a huge camera. Together they walked over to the bales of straw in the middle of the yard and the man fussed around Mr Busby until he was positioned just right. Then, slightly gingerly, he handed him a chicken.

'That chicken's asleep,' Heather commented to Rhona, who replied out of the corner of her mouth, 'Or dead', and indeed it did look very floppy. Then the skinny man started taking photos of the very awkward and uncomfortable-looking Mr Busby.

After about an hour Heather was getting bored. She looked around and saw that the chickens had been put in a sort of pen and were looking really grumpy.

'What's up with you lot?' she asked.

'We've nae been fed. Cooped up in this wee pen, and he's nae even bothered tae feed us.'

'Ah'm starving,' added another crossly.

Heather wandered over to where the bucket was sitting by the fence. It was about half full of corn and she picked up the handle in her mouth.

Rhona was still watching the photographer and Mr Busby. 'I read somewhere that every time someone takes a photograph of you, it captures a bit of your soul. Nonsense, of course, but a bit scary.'

'What's a soul?' asked Heather.

'The part of you that isn't your body. The bit you can't see. Your mind, your memories, your sense of humour. What makes you you. Sort of. Religious people say it's the air that God breathes into every person to make them come alive.'

'Like a balloon?'

'Ish. Christians say your soul goes to heaven when you die, but Buddhists believe that when you die your soul is reborn in another living creature. So you might have been a rabbit before you were a pig. That's why they try never to hurt a living thing, in case it's their granny's soul reborn as something else.'

Heather was utterly baffled. 'A rabbit? Me?'

Rhona grinned at her. 'Rabbit, salmon, horse. Could be anything. Even a daddy-long-legs.'

Heather snorted. 'Don't be silly! Daddy-long-legs are tiny. How would I fit?'

While this conversation had been going on, Heather had put the bucket on the ground by the pen containing the grumpy chickens. She looked around and spotted the scoop the farmer used to put the seed into the bucket. She trotted over and picked it up in her mouth. Then she shovelled up corn in the scoop, rested her front trotters on the top of the pen and started scattering seed for the grateful chickens.

Meanwhile, the man in jeans was looking exasperated.

'It's no good, Bartholomew. This is all so terribly . . .

ordinary. Everyone stay still please.' He spun on his heel, his gimlet eyes roving around the farmyard, and then he stopped. He was staring at Heather, who was still scattering seed to the starving chickens. He raised his hand for quiet, leant forward, brought the camera up to his eye and, in the deathly hush that had fallen over the whole farmyard, he clicked the shutter. Once.

Then he stopped and smiled.

'That pig,' he cried. 'Get the lights on her. Exactly where she is, but with the lights on that hair. I want it glowing. Like a beacon. Like she's on fire!'

People started to bustle about and move lights and someone began washing a very confused Heather while the man in the jeans started taking more photos, his camera clicking and whirring like a sort of friendly rattlesnake.

'Excuse me?' said Mr Busby in a slightly grumpy voice. 'Is this not supposed to be an advertisement for Busby's Birds? Only you seem to be taking pictures of a pig.'

The man tutted as he looked up at the farmer. 'This is about an organic, free-range product, yes?

You're natural? In touch with the animals and what they need? Your chickens are happy chickens?'

'Well, yes,' replied the farmer hesitantly. 'But—'

The man raised his hand. 'I'll be blunt. Free range and organic are not news any more. They are taken for granted. We need something else. Something original. Something unusual. You and a chicken? Honestly? Dull. A place where the animals are farmed by a pig? Memorable, funny and original. It's *Animal Farm* without the politics.'

Mr Busby looked puzzled. 'Animal farm? Is there another kind?'

The photographer looked at him like he was mad. '*Animal Farm*? Famous novel? Pigs take over the farm? Allegory for . . . ? Oh never mind. Just trust me. The pig looks great on camera.'

Chapter 9

Fame
& Freckles

The photographer was right. The advertising
campaign for Busby's Birds was a huge success.
Farmer Busby was overwhelmed. Sales of Busby's
Birds boomed and his pig was a star. You had to hand
it to the photographer in the jeans, he was absolutely
right. A chicken farm run by a pig really caught the
public's imagination. And in Heather, they had their

figurehead. Only she wasn't called Heather. None of them knew that was her name, and anyway they needed her to be called Busby. So that's who she became: Busby Pig, the chicken farmer.

In London Isla saw the adverts and jumped for joy. Although it was a reminder of how desperately she was missing her friend, it was also really nice to see her on the way to school. The posters were huge. In most of them Heather was wearing a flat cap and standing on her hind legs, scattering seed to a farmyard full of hungry, healthy-looking chickens.

The first the animals really knew about it was when Rhona found the same picture in a magazine. There was Heather, her red coat blazing, above a caption saying, *Busby's Birds, bred by experts.*

'It's an advertisement,' explained Rhona. 'For Mr Busby's chickens. Everybody wants natural everything these days, so it'll be to do with that. It's quite clever really; pigs are famously intelligent animals, so they're pretending that you know far more about chickens than a human farmer would.'

Heather looked scared. 'But I don't! I don't know

when their bedtime should be, or what to do if they don't lay properly. How am I going to farm chickens?' Her voice was getting higher and higher as she got more and more panicked and started to turn round and round on the spot.

'Don't worry,' soothed Rhona. 'It's not real. They're only pretending you're the farmer. It's a made-up thing, it's what they do to sell more. You'll see; there'll be more of these all over the place. You may have to do more pictures, but I promise, you won't have to breed any chickens.'

She was right. A week later the animals were playing hide and seek in the barn when a smart sports car drove into the farmyard and a blond woman got out of the front, followed by a Jack Russell terrier. The woman walked over to Farmer Busby and introduced herself.

'Nikki Smith. I've come for the model.'

The farmer looked a bit bemused. 'Model? What model?'

'Busby, of course,' answered Nikki, pointing at Heather. 'The TV campaign is due to start shooting in three days' time so I've come to collect her. I'll have her back in a week or so.'

Mr Busby shrugged. 'Fine by me, but can you not just use any old pig?'

Nikki shook her head. 'It'd be terrible publicity if anyone thought we were cheating. The whole Busby thing would look like we'd made it up.'

'But you have! She's not really a farmer. *I'm* the farmer. She's just a pig. It's all invented!'

The farmer scratched his head in a confused way as the woman walked over to Heather, bent down, stroked her ears and tenderly picked a bit of mud off her back.

'Hello, my name's Nikki and I'm going to be looking after you for the next couple of weeks. Fancy coming to London with me? I'll try to explain everything as we go along, but if you're panicked just squeal. Okay?'

London! Heather felt all her hairs stand up at once. She looked at Rhona and excitedly mouthed, 'Isla! London!' The goat nodded enthusiastically. Heather's mind was racing. This was her chance.

'Shall we go then?' asked Nikki.

Heather got to her feet and turned to the others to say goodbye. Rhona smiled at her supportively and Alastair gazed at her in adoration. At least Heather *thought* he was gazing at her, until she moved and his eyes didn't move with her. She turned her head and saw that the focus of his adoration was actually the little Jack Russell who was sitting quietly at Nikki's feet while her mistress was on the phone.

'She's gorgeous,' panted Alastair, his tongue almost on the floor.

He's got his first crush, thought Heather affectionately as she hopped into the back seat.

That night they all slept in a hotel just off the motorway. Nikki had stayed there before and liked it because the owner didn't mind animals. Heather was far too excited to sleep; she was going to London! To the Isla place! When she could bear it no longer, she nudged the little dog.

'Um, it's Izzy, isn't it?'

'Yup.'

'Only the lady, Nikki, is she your friend? Or your farmer?'

'She's my owner. She got me from a dog's home about two years ago. She's great, and really friendly and nice and in fact I don't know—'

'I'm sorry,' interrupted Heather, 'but she said we were going to London. Is that true?'

'Yup.'

The little dog seemed to jump from being very chatty to not really saying anything very much at all, apart from 'yup'.

Heather pressed on. 'I'm sorry to ask, but why?'

'Because you're famous. In fact, what with you being on posters all over the UK, and now going down to London to do a TV campaign, I'd say you're pretty much a celebrity.'

'No, I'm a pig. A Duroc pig.'

The little dog grinned at her. 'A celebrity is anyone famous. Normally it's only humans who become celebrities, but occasionally it can happen to an animal too. You remember Guy? The gorilla at

London Zoo who died of a heart attack after having a tooth taken out? Animal celebrity. Or Keiko? The killer whale who acted in the film *Free Willy*? Animal celebrity. Laika? The first dog in space? I know everything about celebrities. In fact—'

'Any pigs?' interrupted Heather hesitantly.

'Yup.'

Heather looked at her as if to say 'Go on'. She'd found an apple in a bowl in the room (*Fuji, an attractive modern hybrid apple with a crisp, sweet flavour*) and was chewing as she listened.

'Obviously the Tamworth Two,' said Izzy, and then, seeing Heather's blank look, she shuffled a bit closer. 'A brother and sister pair of Tamworths were on their way to be slaughtered when they escaped through a hedge and then swam over a river. They were on the run for a week before they were spotted foraging in someone's garden, shot with tranquiliser guns and recaptured. They're retired now. There was Pigasus. He was a joke candidate for the 1968 US presidential election. And of course LuLu the Vietnamese pot-bellied pig. Her owner had a heart attack and LuLu lay down in the road until a car stopped and then grabbed hold of the driver's coat and wouldn't let go until her owner had been rescued.'

'So am I one of them?' gulped Heather nervously.

'Sort of. You're a model. You pose for pictures. Or you have done. Hitherto. Now we're going to London because they want to shoot a follow-up TV advertisement so we need to be in a studio.'

Izzy chattered away and Heather started to drift off, thinking about what the next few days would bring. In one sleep's time, or maybe two, they would be in London. The exact place Isla was. So lucky! Then all she had to do was escape from Nikki and find Isla. It couldn't be that hard. How many little girls with freckles could there be in London?

Chapter 10

Elephants & Castles

The next afternoon they reached the outskirts of London and Heather started to scout for Isla. Nikki had taken the roof off the top of the car and Heather and Izzy were quite enjoying the wind whistling through their hair as they zoomed along. About twenty minutes later, when they'd driven past about a thousand houses and at least ten schools, Heather started to realise the size of her task.

'Izzy?' asked Heather tentatively. 'Do a lot of people live in London?'

'Yup.'

'How many?'

'About seven million, I think. Why?'

Heather gulped. 'I just thought it would be smaller. How does anyone find their way around?'

'With difficulty. Apparently more people get lost in London than any other city in the world. And one in three Londoners freely admit they give people the wrong directions. It's not a very friendly place. We probably should have stayed in Scotland,' concluded the little dog cheerily.

As Heather looked out at all the cars whizzing past – horns blaring, people leaning out of their windows and shouting at each other – she felt a very, very long way from her friend, and even further from her beloved farm. She feared even the apples would taste different.

'Ooh look, a thing like a castle on top of an

elephant. That's funny,' said Izzy, gazing out the other side of the car.

Something went off inside Heather's head. She knew it was important, but why? She squirmed round and saw what Izzy was talking about. A building with a model of an elephant and a castle in front. Elephant and Castle! That was in the letter! Isla's letter! Isla!

'Izzy! You've got to help me! I've got to get out!'

'Why? What's wrong?'

'Just . . . please!'

'Do you need the loo?'

'Of course not, I went before we left.'

'Only, Nikki always lets me out if I need the loo.'

Heather's brain was racing. She surreptitiously crossed her trotters, took a deep breath and lied. 'I mean yes, I need the loo! I'm desperate!'

Izzy barked three times, like a code, and Nikki instantly pulled over to the side of the road and hopped out of the car. She opened the back door and unbuckled Izzy. Heather grunted at her and Nikki undid her belt as well.

'You as well? Come on then, both of you.'

She helped them out and led them to the kerb in front of the car.

Heather looked at the road but everything was going really fast, so she turned and looked the other way. There were loads of people but it seemed safer, so she took a deep breath, stamped on Nikki's foot to distract her, felt really guilty and ran. Behind her Nikki howled in pain and was hopping up and down on one foot shouting, 'Busby! Busby!' but Heather was gone. She was going her fastest, ears pressed flat against her head as she galloped, swerving in and out of the people walking towards her, eyes scanning ahead to see what obstacles were coming.

She skidded to a halt at a main road, and turned sideways to face a scary sort of tunnel that seemed to go under the road. With Nikki's voice shouting 'Stop! Izzy, follow her! Catch her!' from behind, she had no choice. She bolted down into the opening. She ran into a sort of tunnel which then opened out into a sort of room underground. There were five other openings and Heather plumped for the one in the middle. She ran up it and came out into daylight again. She looked around and saw she was on a sort of island with cars going all around her. Across the road she could see Nikki scanning frantically. Heather felt really bad but she couldn't explain to Nikki that she had something really important to do. Suddenly there was barking from behind her and there was Izzy. Nikki heard her and looked over. Her eyes met Heather's across the traffic. She looked so worried and sad Heather almost gave up, but she remembered another pair of eyes, ones that reminded her of Coco Pops, and she knew she had to go on. She turned to Izzy.

'I've got to go. I'm really sorry and I hope Nikki doesn't get into trouble, but I've got to find someone. She's my best human friend and I know she's here somewhere. I wouldn't go if it wasn't really important. Do you understand?'

'Yup.'

And Heather ran.

Nikki's cries were ringing in her ears as Heather

twisted and turned without any idea where she was headed. She had no sense of direction in this huge, noisy city, and then she smelt something. It was like rotten fruit, and as she had nothing else to guide her, she thought she might as well follow her snout. It led her down an alley and around a corner to where a man in a cap and tattoos was standing in front of a sort of set of shelves on wheels loaded with delicious-looking fruit and veg.

She cast her expert eye over three types of mushroom, gleaming potatoes, shiny leeks, bobbly-skinned avocados, crisp cauliflowers and oh oh oh, juicy, moist, earth-flecked carrots. Her stomach roared with hunger and she sat down with a bump, her mouth suddenly filled with saliva. In a daze she stared and grunted hungrily. The man spotted her and shooed her away. She ignored him, so he picked up an apple (*Sweet Alford, pinkish flesh, excellent eating*) and threw it at her head. She caught it expertly and within two bites it was gone.

The tattooed man walked towards her. 'Go on! Get out of it!' and as she reluctantly sidled off he threw an onion after her. She'd never been keen on onions, so she caught it, and then very politely put it down on the ground and snouted it back to him.

The man looked gobsmacked, but a customer was watching and said, 'Try a sprout.' The tattooed man grabbed a handful of sprouts and started firing them at Heather like a machine gun. Heather jumped left and right, up and down, catching the sprouts in her mouth, not missing a single one. By now a small crowd had gathered to watch the agile pig twisting and turning.

'Isn't that the pig from the adverts? You know, Busby?' said one little boy, pulling at his dad's coat.

'It does look like him, you're right; but it can't be. Must just be the same breed,' answered the dad. He reached out and gave the tattooed man a pound coin. Then he picked up an avocado and gave it to his son, indicating that he should give it to Heather. The boy walked over cautiously and held out the avocado. Heather delicately bit into it, chewed and then walked to a pile of rubbish under the cart and expertly spat the stone on top of the rubbish. Everyone laughed and other people started buying more and more things for her to eat. This went on all day, and by the time Heather fell fast asleep that evening, she had a terrible tummy ache.

Chapter 11

Rhubarb & Mustard

Heather slept where the man parked his stall. He tried to take her home with him, but Heather refused. Isla was somewhere near here – she wasn't going anywhere. In the morning the man came back, gently nudged her awake and gave her an apple (*Jazz, crisp flesh with a rich, peardrop flavour*) for her breakfast. Jazz apples were a particular favourite of Heather's and just what she needed to start her day. Perhaps London wasn't so bad after all.

For the next few sleeps she split her time between walking around searching for Isla, and making sure she had enough energy by eating whatever the man offered her. On the third day, the man excitedly showed her a picture of the two of them in the newspaper. There was his stall and there was Heather, head up, gulping down a long stalk of rhubarb like a sword-swallower, while a crowd looked on. The caption under the picture read *Pigging out*, and the tattoed man told her excitedly that someone had taken the picture the day before and it would be great for his business. He was so pleased he pointed to his stall as if to say, 'Take your pick' and Heather thought long and hard before choosing a particularly delicious-looking iceberg lettuce.

She was crunching away at her lettuce and thinking that Izzy would have approved of her being in the paper – she'd warmed to the little dog and was feeling bad about having run out on her –

when she got the shock of her life. Isla! Walking along on the other side of the road! She was walking away from her so Heather couldn't see her face, but the jacket was definitely the one Isla had been wearing in the picture she'd drawn, so was the skirt, and the hair was long and brown. She was walking along with a man who Heather didn't know. Maybe this was Uncle Max?

Her lettuce forgotten, Heather leapt to her feet and galloped straight across the road.

CRASH! A bicycle slammed into her flank, a car swerved to avoid the bicycle which went straight into the barrow of fruit, while the car hit a rubbish bin and then a lamppost. Heather was knocked sideways and rolled over and over before stopping when she hit the opposite pavement. A man got out of the car looking dazed and went to check the front of the car, which was wrapped around the lamppost like a roll around a sausage. The bicyclist was ruefully picking himself up out of the fruit stall where he'd landed face first in the tomatoes while the stallholder waved his fist at the splattered cyclist.

'Bleeding road hog! What you doing going that fast?'

The cyclist looked around in angry bewilderment. 'Road hog? Me? That pig came out of nowhere. Why wasn't it on a lead?'

Heather, meanwhile, was getting groggily to her feet and looking around for Isla. She was alarmed to see the girl disappearing around the corner. She looked back at the mayhem she'd caused, thought *Sorry* a bit, and then set off in hot pursuit.

Her right front trotter was sore, and she knew she'd have a bruise on her flank in the morning, but she had her goal in sight and she limped after the little girl as fast as she could go. She was moving slowly though and the gap was widening until luck smiled on Heather. A traffic light went red and the girl was stuck waiting for the green man to reappear so she could cross the street. Heather reached her side, wheezed a bit, and then gripped Isla's skirt firmly in her jaws and gave it a massive tug.

The little girl looked down and screamed, jumping back towards her dad. It wasn't Isla at all, and in her shock Heather's jaw froze and she couldn't let go of the skirt. The girl was still shrieking and the man reached over with his umbrella and gave Heather a good whack right on the tip of her snout. That did the trick. She yelped in agony and the little girl got her skirt back. Heather retreated, her eyes watering with pain, and the man and the girl fled across the road.

Heather was devastated. Her snout was throbbing, she ached where the bicycle had hit her, her trotter was sore and she was utterly downhearted. She sank down and for the first time it hit her how impossible her task was. How could she have imagined that she would find one girl in the middle of this huge and daunting place? She shuffled into a nearby garden where there was a very large bush. It was a bit prickly but Heather didn't care any more. She crawled under the middle of it so she was hidden from passers-by, rested her bruised snout on her battered trotters and cried. And once she'd started she couldn't stop. She had never felt more depressed and less happy. Why had she left the farm? Why had she run away from

Nikki? Why wasn't Isla here? She was lost, alone and had nothing left.

After a while the bawling turned to hiccupy sobs and then eventually petered out altogether. Heather was at rock bottom but, as so often happens, when you reach rock bottom the only way is up, and so it proved for Heather. Just when she thought she might as well give in, she witnessed a sort of miracle.

She saw Isla walking along the opposite pavement. And then she saw a second Isla walking just behind the first. And then a third Isla drove past in the passenger seat of a car. A bus drew up and four more Islas got off the bus. Everywhere she looked there were Islas, all identically dressed, and all heading in the same direction.

In a daze Heather got to her feet and set off after them. She crossed the road, more carefully this time, and went round a corner to see all the Islas converging on one place. They were all going through a gate in a fence, behind which was a big open space where they all seemed to be gathering together. Heather walked over to the fence and stared through the wire at the hundreds of Islas all running about. There were tall ones, short ones, skinny ones, plump ones, dark-haired ones, blond ones, spiky, curly – all looking like the Isla in the drawing, but none of them exactly right. None of them quite—

'Heather Duroc?'

Heather spun round and there she was. Her Isla, the real Isla, the only Isla, dressed like all the others, but different. Taller than she'd been when Heather last saw her; she'd lost one of her front teeth so there was a big gap where it should have been, but there were the same sparkling eyes, the same lopsided smile, and even more freckles.

Heather lurched forward and poor Isla was nearly knocked over as two hundred pounds of pig snuffled into her and demanded to be stroked and petted.

'Why are you here? *How* are you here? How did you find me? I saw the poster and you were called Busby and I knew it was you, although Dad wasn't sure, but I said it was so you and what are you doing here? I've missed you so much. Did you get my letter? I'm sorry it was so sad, but I was just not very happy and I so wanted to see you and this is my school. It's a bit better now but it's still nowhere near as nice as Old Meldrum. How did you get here? I've got so much to tell you, but it's school now so I have to go in and I don't think you'd better come. Wait here and I'll bring you a snack at lunchtime and then we can talk afterwards. Will you wait for me? Scrunch if that's a good plan.'

Heather looked up at the girl and scrunched her snout like she'd never scrunched before. Isla grinned at her and then in the distance a bell rang and she looked panicked.

'That's school starting. Quick, hide in this garden and I'll come and find you later. If anyone comes out, just duck behind the bins and wait for me.' She reached into her bag and produced a lunchbox. She opened it up and took out an apple and a sandwich. She peered between the slices of bread, made an 'oops' face, and took something pink out of the middle before giving Heather the bread and the apple (*Northern Lights, glossy bright-red fruit with slightly tart flesh*). 'There you are, that's all I've got, so that'll just have to keep you going until I can get to the tuck shop later. There's mustard in the sandwich so be careful!' She bent down and gave Heather a kiss on her snout. Then she shouldered her bag and ran through the gates into the place full of Islas.

Chapter 12

Crisps
& Camouflage

Heather had never felt happier. Finding Isla was even better than not being apart in the first place! She hid in the garden all day, terrified that someone was going to discover her and take her away. Isla popped out at lunchtime and gave Heather a packet of crisps, and then at three-thirty she raced out and the two of them scampered off to the park together.

'I still can't believe you're here. I haven't been able to concentrate all day. Miss Grey kept asking me if I was feeling okay – I was grinning so much – and I kept getting the maths questions wrong and I'm normally really good at them. We should be walking back with Martha and her au pair because her mum works in an optician's, but I told them I was meeting a friend from Scotland so not to worry about me which wasn't a complete lie, you're just not a human friend! Shall we get an ice cream? I was so excited when I saw the posters going up and I said to Dad he should *so* recognise you because he was your farmer – double ninety-nine with two flakes, please – and that cap you wear in the adverts quite suits you although it's a bit freaky seeing you standing on your back legs – thanks – here, you have first lick.'

They ate the ice cream as they wandered home and Isla let herself into the flat with her key. She whispered to Heather that there was someone in the flat called Mrs Maatens. 'She's a Dutch lady and her children are all grown-up so she looks after me from when school ends until Dad comes home. She's very deaf and I think she might be a bit scared of you so we won't tell her you're here.'

Isla went into the kitchen to say hello and Heather tiptoed to where Isla pointed was her room. Isla came in a minute later carrying some yogurts. They had a little feast and Isla chatted away as if they'd never been apart.

When they heard her dad come back, Isla put her finger on her lips and got Heather to hide in the wardrobe. 'Let's surprise him.' They could hear her dad saying goodbye to Mrs Maatens and then he came into Isla's room while she pretended to be reading on the bed. He looked very serious and sat down next to Isla.

'You're not going to want to hear this, love. It's about Busby – I mean, Heather.'

Isla grinned at him, she couldn't stop herself. 'I know, I know, she's escaped and—'

He put his hand up and he looked so sad and serious she went quiet.

'Dad, what's wrong?'

He couldn't look her in the eye. 'Nobody knows

where she is, but they're very worried. It seems she's gone a bit . . . well, a bit . . . mad, I suppose. Someone called me and asked if I knew anything about it. Seems she ran away from the person who was taking her to the television studio to make another advert and now she's on the loose somewhere in London.'

He took out the paper and showed Isla the picture of Heather eating rhubarb. 'Look, that's the fruit and veg man on Marchmont Street. They're desperate to find her; they're saying she's really dangerous.'

Isla couldn't listen any more. 'She's not mad, she's fine, Dad. I know she is. They've got it all wrong. You don't believe them, do you?'

The ex-farmer shook his head sadly. 'I'm sorry, love. Apparently she went mad, attacked a cyclist, caused a massive pile-up, ruined that man's fruit stall and then tried to bite a St Anthony's girl on her way to school! They're saying she's got swine flu and that is really serious. They've got the people from Pest Control out looking for her and everything. I know she was your friend, my love, but she's also a wild animal.'

'But what will they do to her if they find her? Will they send her home?'

The farmer looked serious. 'Sometimes when animals get ill like that they don't know what they're doing. When that happens it's usually best to gently put them out of their misery so they don't suffer any more. She won't feel a thing. She probably won't even know what's happening. I'm sorry, love; I know how fond you were of her.'

'But swine flu can kill you. She hasn't got it, has she?'

The ex-farmer pulled his daughter into his chest and gave her a big hug. 'I'd be very surprised if she did. None of my animals ever caught it and I haven't heard of any cases for ages, but who knows? Perhaps she has. Try not to think about it. I know it's been a difficult year but I promise things will get better soon.'

'Dad? If she did, um, you know, wherever she is, if she did have it, how could you tell? I mean, if you saw her?'

The farmer looked puzzled. 'She'd have a fever, probably sneeze a bit and have a cough like a dog barking. She might also be gummy around the eyes and she'd probably be tired and not hungry. Why?'

Isla said nothing, but if her dad could have seen her eyes he'd have been alarmed at the determined glint in them. The moment he left she opened the wardrobe and climbed in next to Heather. She got her torch out and turned it on. She put it on the floor, shining upwards, which made them both look a bit spooky, and then she took Heather's face between her hands and looked at her very seriously.

Isla took a deep breath. 'I know you can understand me and I've got to ask you this question. Swine flu makes you cough and get a fever, so are you feeling coughy or hot?'

At that precise moment some of the dust in the wardrobe got up Heather's snout and she gave a huge sneeze.

Isla looked at her in alarm and picked up the torch. She shone it at Heather's eyes which made the pig blink and her eyes water. Isla reached for her school bag and pulled out a packet of crisps. She shut her eyes and offered them to Heather.

Heather had no hesitation at all – she was starving and she stuck her snout right into the packet of crisps, tipped it up in the air and let all the crisps fall into her open, waiting mouth. Then she licked the packet. Then she stuck her snout into Isla's school bag where she found an apple core (*Keepsake, fine-grained, hard, very crisp with juicy light yellow flesh*), an empty packet of raisins and some sweet wrappers. She gobbled them all up and then looked back at her friend in a 'Have you got anything else?' sort of way.

Isla beamed at her. 'No loss of appetite then. I knew you didn't have it. Listen, we know there's nothing wrong with you, but nobody's going to believe that now. We've got to get you somewhere safe. You can stay in here tonight and in the morning we'll work something out.'

The next day Isla explained to Heather they needed to find somewhere safe to hide her while she went to school, but in the meantime they worked out an escape route and an early warning system in case Heather had to make a sudden run for it. Isla made sure the window was always open about a snout's height. There were books on the floor which looked higgledy-piggledy but were actually a sort of staircase, so that if Heather needed to escape she could clamber up the books, onto the desk, snout the window open and jump out to the garden outside. The only tricky bit was snouting the window but they practised and practised until she could do it quickly, easily and quietly.

If Isla wasn't in the room with Heather when someone came looking, she would say, 'My room's so messy, it's like a pigsty!' at the top of her voice and that would be Heather's cue to escape into the garden until Isla could give her the all-clear.

Isla looked down at her friend, at the trusting eyes staring up at her, one trotter resting on Isla's leg as they shared a banana.

She said, 'There's something else we've got to do. You're currently the most famous pig in Britain. People know you from newspaper adverts and your face is on posters everywhere. We've got to stop people noticing you. We need to turn you into a stick insect. We need camouflage.'

That night, Isla was lying in bed with the light out when her dad put his head round the door for a final check.

'Dad?'

'I thought you were asleep. What's up?'

'Can I paint my room, please?'

'Why? What's wrong with it?'

'Nothing, I just want it to feel more like mine. Like I've chosen it. Like it's my space, you know? I'll get Mrs M to take me to the hardware shop tomorrow. Get some samples.'

'Okay, sleep well.' He blew her a kiss and shut the door.

Chapter 13

My Bedroom's a Pigsty!

The next afternoon, Isla took Mrs Maatens to the hardware store and bought sample pots of paint. Mrs Maatens was a little worried by Isla's choice of five different shades of black and two of pink, and she resolved to have a word with Mr Wolstenholme when he got home.

When they got in, Isla settled Mrs Maatens in

front of the telly with a cup of tea and a biscuit and then set to work. She put plenty of newspaper down on the floor of her bedroom, wedged the chair under the door handle, arranged Heather in front of the full-length mirror on the door of the wardrobe and got going. She shook the little paint tins and then laid them all out in a line.

'They're different shades because, obviously, I could only get one of each, but I'll try and make you sort of the same all over. I nearly got water soluble but then I thought you might be out in the rain and then it'd all wash off and that would be a disaster.'

Isla put her tongue between her teeth, like she did when she was concentrating really hard, took a deep breath, cracked open the first pot, dipped her brush and started to paint.

Thirty minutes later she'd finished the first coat. Heather looked completely different. She was now a mixture of Infinite Black, Jet Black, Creosote Black and a little bit of Volcanic Grey. Isla stepped back and admired her handiwork. 'I'll paint some pink splotches on when this coat has properly dried. You'll look like a proper Saddleback pig by the time I'm done.'

Heather wasn't sure she liked the sound of being a Saddleback, although she didn't mind being painted. It felt quite like mud after a really good roll, sort of a mixture of wet and heavy at the same time. She grunted happily and Isla gave her a big grin. Then her face changed and she started looking serious.

'I've been thinking about what we should do. We urgently need to find somewhere you can hide out until everyone forgets about you. I just don't know where.' At that moment the doorbell went. 'Don't move, you're still very wet,' whispered Isla, opening the bedroom door.

'It's all right, Mrs M,' she shouted as she passed the sitting room, 'I'll get it.' The deaf lady had the television on so loud it was a wonder the neighbours hadn't complained. She certainly hadn't heard the doorbell, and Isla grinned. Given the volume of the telly, it was something of a miracle she'd heard it herself.

She put the chain on the front door and opened it to reveal a man with a dog and a blond woman wearing a T-shirt saying, *Proud to be a Busby Bird*. She had a little dog at her feet, too.

'Isla Wolstenholme?' said the woman carefully.

'Yes,' replied Isla equally carefully.

The man held out a card with his photo above the words, *Horatio Hornbuckle – Pest Control and Termination Operative*.

The woman carried on speaking. 'My name's Nikki and this is Horatio. My dog is called Izzy, his dog is Thomas. We're here about Busby the pig. We're looking for her everywhere and I gather you knew her before she was famous. Could we come in please?'

'No!' said Isla rather too sharply. 'You can't come in because my dad's not here.'

Nikki looked concerned. 'Are you all alone?'

'No, Mrs Maatens is looking after me but she's deaf. You'll have to come back tomorrow.'

Nikki looked a bit puzzled, but at that precise moment Mr Wolstenholme arrived behind them and, seeing Isla at the door, asked what was going on. As Nikki introduced herself and explained what they were doing, Isla was getting more and more nervous and fidgety, desperate to get away and warn her friend. Nikki had finished explaining and Mr Wolstenholme was looking a bit cross as he motioned for Isla to take the chain off the door and let him in.

'I'm getting heartily sick of all this pig stuff,' he said. He stepped inside the door and put his arm around Isla firmly. 'First my daughter's head teacher tells me it's not safe for Isla to go to school alone, and now we're being bothered at home. Could you just do your job, catch the flaming pig and then we can all get on with our lives?'

Nikki nodded apologetically. 'We just wanted a quick word. We wondered if you'd seen or heard anything that might give us a clue as to Busby's whereabouts. Could we . . . um?' She indicated inside the house and Mr Wolstenholme sighed and opened the door wide.

As they came in, Mr Hornbuckle's dog lowered his nose to the ground and sniffed. He was a dachshund, so he was already fairly close to the ground and you almost didn't notice when he lowered his head. He barked once.

Mr Hornbuckle turned to the ex-farmer. 'Have you got any pets?'

Mr Wolstenholme shook his head.

The pest controller put his head on one side and gazed at him quizzically.

'Really? There are definite traces of animal here somewhere,' he said, looking down at his dog. 'Thomas has detected something, and Thomas is seldom, if ever, mistaken. Mind if I take a look around?'

He didn't wait for a response and headed straight into the kitchen. Isla was jumping up and down frantically and Nikki looked at her thoughtfully before turning to her dog. 'Izzy, why don't you go and wait for me in the car?' The little dog disappeared and Nikki turned back to Isla. 'I think we need to go in, don't we?'

Meanwhile, inside Isla's room, Heather was peacefully standing on the newspaper waiting for her new coat to dry. She could see herself in the mirror and decided she looked rather smart, although she might have preferred to be all one shade of black rather than slightly patchy. Still, maybe it would be better when Isla put some pink on her. Where was Isla anyway? She'd been ages. Heather decided to go and listen more closely at the door, to see if she could hear anything other than the television. When she tried to move, though, she found she couldn't lift her trotters. They must have got paint under them, because all four of them were stuck firmly to the newspaper. At that very moment, the noise from the television went off and her heart nearly stopped as she heard Isla's voice urgently shouting the code just outside the door, 'But my room's far too messy, in fact, it's a pigsty!'

Outside her bedroom, Isla was almost frantic as Mr Hornbuckle and Thomas sniffed their way around the flat, getting closer and closer to her room. Every once in a while the dog would stop and bark and his master would drop to the floor, pick up something tiny and hold it up to the light before smiling in a satisfied way, popping it into a little plastic bottle and getting back on the trail. They were speeding up now; they ignored the living room and were heading straight towards her as she stood blocking the path to her bedroom door.

Both man and dog were concentrating so hard that they didn't notice she was there, and the man's head was so low as he followed his dog that he only stopped when the dog went between Isla's planted feet and the top of the man's head bumped into her tummy. He looked up, slightly puzzled, and stretched past Isla to open the door to her bedroom. Isla moved to block him. He moved sideways and she moved with him. He moved the other way and again Isla blocked him. He dodged back but she was too fast for him; he pretended to go one way but Isla guessed what he was doing and thwarted him again. Finally an exasperated Mr Wolstenholme intervened.

'Let the man in, Isla. The sooner he sees your room,

the sooner he can be done and leave us in peace.'

Isla shook her head; she had tears in her eyes and didn't trust herself to speak, but she wasn't going to give in. She clutched at the door frame and then, just as both her dad and Mr Hornbuckle stepped forward to move her, another voice spoke. Nikki had been watching Isla all this time and now she put her hand on the man's shoulder.

'Horatio, we don't need to see inside her room. Busby's hardly going to be in a girl's bedroom now, is she?' She gently but firmly turned the man around and propelled him and his dog back along the hall towards the doorway. Isla and Mr Wolstenholme followed and when they all got to the door, Nikki turned round and shook Mr Wolstenholme's hand.

'So sorry to have bothered you, and thank you for your time.' Then she bent down and, making sure that nobody else could see, she gave Isla a big wink. 'Goodbye, Isla.' She said it slowly before adding very deliberately, 'You don't need to worry about Busby. I'm sure she won't bother anyone again. Perhaps she's gone somewhere she'll never be found. Like a safari park, for instance, or even the zoo.'

Mr Hornbuckle was giving his dog a sweet from a packet and looking rather sad. He got to his feet, and as Isla was grinning at Nikki, the man saw his chance. He ducked around the two of them, strode along the corridor to Isla's room with the dog scuttling behind him, and grabbed the door handle. Isla shouted 'No!' and Nikki gasped in horror as they watched the man turn the door handle decisively. Nikki grabbed Isla's hand and they ran to join Mr Hornbuckle. He flung the door open and the three of them burst into the room.

Chapter 14

Moving Bushes & Breaking Eggs

It was chaos. Spilt paint pots, books all over the floor, clothes everywhere and a chair knocked over on its side. And there, in the corner of the room, under the window, was a single sheet of newspaper covered in black and grey paint and with four holes in it – one in each corner and each one about the size of a trotter. Above it the window was open and a gentle breeze was blowing through it, ruffling the newspaper. Other than that the room was empty.

Heather was gone.

'This room really is a pigsty!' said Nikki disapprovingly. Isla looked embarrassed, but she was so relieved that Heather had escaped that she couldn't mind too much. Thomas the dachshund was sniffing frantically, his nose twitching as if it was full of pepper. He stopped, barked once, then twice and started sniffing along the carpet. Mr Hornbuckle let himself be pulled along as the dog led him to the newspaper, up the books stacked into stairs and over to the window. They both climbed up onto the desk and then sort of flowed out of the window, almost as if both man and dog were made of melted plastic. Isla looked at Nikki who grinned at her and tapped the side of her head in a gesture which clearly meant, 'He's a bit nuts.' Then they both followed him into the garden where the man and dog were both snuffling around the grass in wider and wider circles.

Out of the corner of her eye Isla saw the bush in the middle of the garden move, and she was sure she could see a trotter poking out of the bottom. Mr Hornbuckle had dropped to the ground and was inching forward on his hands and knees. As he got closer and closer to the bush, Isla panicked. She had to do something!

'Dad! Help!'

Mr Wolstenholme stuck his head out of her window and looked at the very bizarre scene in the communal garden. He clambered out, walked over to Mr Hornbuckle, stood directly in front of him and coughed. Mr Hornbuckle looked up, half curious and half cross.

'Could you get up, please?' said Mr Wolstenholme.

The pest operative did as he was told.

'I've had enough of this. I would like you to go away and leave us alone.' The ex-farmer sounded very calm, but Isla knew that tone of voice.

'But there's been a pig here! My dog can smell it. Even I can smell it! That girl is lying!' protested the man as he pointed at Isla.

Mr Wolstenholme clenched his fists and took a deep breath.

'I'm not a violent man, but say that one more time and you could change me.'

As Nikki put her hand on Mr Hornbuckle's shoulder and gently ushered him away, Mr Wolstenholme turned to Isla. 'So, missy, are you going to tell me what this is all about?'

'Nothing, Daddy, promise!' said Isla, with her fingers firmly crossed behind her back.

'Why are you calling me Daddy? You never call me Daddy. What's going on? And why is that bush moving?' He started to head towards the bush, which was undoubtedly moving.

'Stop!'

Her dad looked at her very oddly.

'I'm starving – can you make me a special omelette? You know, the really good ones where you break the eggs! The ones you call your special omelettes. I'm sure Nikki would like one too. Nikki? Would you like one of my dad's special omelettes? They're really, um . . . special.' Isla was gabbling now as Nikki came back into the garden, having got rid of Mr Hornbuckle.

'That sounds lovely,' answered Nikki with a grin. She fixed the ex-farmer with a dazzling smile. 'If it's not too much trouble.'

Mr Wolstenholme looked a bit flustered. 'No! No trouble at all. That's fine. Right. Yes. Of course,' he answered in a daze, heading back towards the flat.

Nikki followed him and as they went inside she winked at Isla. 'See you in a minute,' she said.

The moment she'd gone, Isla rushed over to the bush and extracted the quivering, grass- and leaf-covered Heather from her hiding place. Together they scrambled back through the bedroom window and Isla tried to pick off the worst of the things that had got stuck to the drying paint before helping Heather into the wardrobe and shutting the door.

The next morning, Isla was ill. She wasn't really, but when her dad came in to wake her up, she pretended to be feeling poorly and said she was tired and didn't want to go to school. Her dad looked at her strangely and then agreed that she could stay in bed. He said he had to go to the office in the morning but he'd be back at lunchtime, and he left her his mobile phone just in case she was feeling too ill to get to the phone.

The moment he was gone, Isla leapt out of bed and ran to the wardrobe. She opened it and a very bedraggled-looking Heather shuffled out. Isla got her a bowl of milk and an apple (*Seek-No-Further, creamy yellow flesh streaked red, with an aromatic tender taste*) and while Heather ate her breakfast, Isla picked off some more leaves and told her what had gone on after she'd been wardrobed.

'So then Dad made us all omelettes and nice Nikki said that Mr Hornbuckle – that's the pest man – was really worried, especially because you'd bitten that girl, and Mr Busby'd told him you'd got swine flu, but Nikki reckoned that was rubbish and it was only Anaya Postlethwaite who said that, and she's not even in my class, but now they're looking all over for you and I really wanted to tell Nikki about you being here, but I didn't because I don't know her, and even though she said you'd probably gone to the zoo, I think she knew you had been here and she was trying to tell me that's what we should do, because she said it again just before she left, so if you finish your milk we can sneak out and smuggle you into the zoo.'

As she was talking, she picked up her piggy bank and tipped out the contents. Heather finished her milk and they went out of Isla's room, closing the door behind them. Isla was by the front door, putting her coat on, when to her horror she heard a key turning in the lock and a familiar voice calling through it.

'Helloh?'

It was Mrs Maatens!

Heather galloped back towards Isla's room as Isla pulled the hall table in front of the door and then raced down the corridor after her friend and dived into her bedroom. They could hear Mrs Maatens making a huge noise and fuss as she pushed the front door open and then started shuffling towards Isla's room. Isla shoved Heather into the wardrobe, slammed it shut, pulled off her fleece and jumped into bed, pulling the covers right up to her chin just as the grey head of Mrs Maatens appeared around her door.

'Helloh, little Iseller.' Mrs Maatens could never pronounce her name properly. 'Your pappy asked me to pop in and keep my eye out for you before he comes back for lunchtime. I hope I didn't wake you with the noise, only there was a table that must have fallen over by the front door, stopping me coming in.'

Isla's heart was racing as Mrs Maatens came into her room, sat down on the bed and put her hand on her forehead.

'Oh, you poor thing. You're all hot and sweaty and you're panting like a puppy. Stay there and I'll get you a nice glass of milk. And some cheese, perhaps? I remember my mother always used to say, "Cheese for a fever, cabbage for a cold." Or was it the other way around? Perhaps—'

Isla frantically interrupted her. 'Actually, Mrs M, I think I'd just like to go to sleep, you know? I'll call you when I wake up. But thank you anyway.'

Mrs Maatens stood up and then she noticed Isla's fleece where it had been chucked on the floor. She picked it up and underneath it was Heather's bowl of milk. Mrs Maatens looked at it very curiously while

Isla struggled to think of something to say. Then Mrs Maatens folded the fleece and before Isla could do anything, she walked over to the wardrobe and opened the door . . .

Heather was cowering in the wardrobe, listening to Mrs Maatens chatting away to Isla, when she heard footsteps approaching and then watched in horror as the wardrobe door was opened, the coat-hangers were pushed to one side and Mrs Maatens peered in and saw a black-painted, grass-covered pig staring back at her. Heather smiled nervously and Mrs Maatens screamed, dropped the fleece and fainted.

Isla was out of bed in a flash and quickly helped Heather out of the wardrobe and through the window. 'Wait for me in the garden,' she whispered, and then turned back to Mrs Maatens who was lying on the floor, unconscious. What should she do? She put a pillow under the lady's head, but how could she wake her up? Smelling salts, that's what people always used. She didn't have any of them, but she ran to the kitchen, opened the fridge and got out a really stinky piece of cheese. Holding her breath, she scurried back to her bedroom and held it under Mrs Maatens's nose until the Dutch lady gasped and woke up.

'A pig! There was a pig in your cupboard. I saw it!' she said with real horror in her voice. 'Right there, staring at me with big eyes. A pig! One of those big, black pigs with huge teeth! Horrid!'

Isla helped her sit up and walked over to the wardrobe. She opened it wide. 'There's nothing there, Mrs M. You must have imagined it. I do that sort of thing all the time. Maybe you should watch the telly while I have a sleep.'

Mrs Maatens got to her feet and tiptoed cautiously over to the wardrobe. She peered suspiciously inside, looked behind all the clothes and nervously opened all the drawers, but she did have to admit there was no pig there. She tutted to herself and went out of the room. Isla breathed a huge sigh of relief and flopped back on the bed until she heard the noise of the television. Then she put a bundle of clothes under the covers to look like she was in bed, grabbed the phone her dad had given her, slipped out of the window, and she and Heather set off.

Chapter 15

Old Meldrum Mayhem

'. . . Because I Googled the zoo yesterday and Nikki's absolutely right, it's the perfect place to hide you. There's every kind of animal there so you'll just blend in. And it's really easy to get there so I can come and visit you all the time. It's just on the Tube, which I've used loads of times before because London's so big it's really hard to get anywhere if you don't. And it's weird, because there's so many people here but nobody ever really notices anybody else. I mean, if you and me were walking around in Aberdeen, people would say something. Probably, "Why aren't you in school?" or, "What's happened to that pig? Why've you painted her black?" But here nobody really talks to anyone else. Dad says it's sad because people are all rushing and don't look around and take in what an amazing place this is. I mean, don't get me wrong, I really miss the countryside, but this is such a cool place because you can do and see pretty much anything if you look hard enough. Even a girl going to the zoo with her best friend who's a Duroc pig!' Isla grinned at Heather, who snuffled happily.

They went into a building, through some gates and down a moving staircase. Isla had put a bit of string around Heather's neck and she held it tight. 'Look, this is the Tube. Don't be scared of it, it's just like a really long caterpillar. We get inside it . . .'

Isla had been talking since they left home, which did attract a few funny looks, but as she'd pointed out, nobody actually stopped her or asked her where she was going. When they got to the zoo, Isla made Heather hide while she went to investigate getting inside. She went up to one of the ticket lines and asked the man how much it cost to get in.

She was back five minutes later, looking determined.

'Okay. There's good news and bad. I can't afford to buy a ticket, I'm too young to go in on my own, and pets aren't allowed in at all.'

Heather sat very still. What was the good news?

'The good news is that we're here and I'm not leaving until you're safely inside. I had a look at the map on the guide and I reckon we need to get in round the back, by the petting zoo. As far as I remember, the fence by the camels is a bit lower, so we'll go round there and get you sorted out, then I'll work out some way to get inside and come and help you over the fence. There are some regular pigs just by the camels and then there are some Bearded pigs just by Tiger Territory. We'll see which is the better place to hide you once we're inside. Oh, and there are zookeepers everywhere so we'll have to be extra sneaky. They wear green sweatshirts, so watch out for them. When we get inside, try to look small. Scrunch if that sounds like a plan.'

Heather gulped and did a sort of half scrunch, which she hoped Isla would understand meant she was okay but a little nervous. She had faith in her friend though, particularly when Isla was this determined.

Isla grinned and produced an apple from her pocket (*Granny Smith, the most instantly recognisable of all apples – green with a clean, acidic flavour*), which she lobbed up into the air. Heather opened her mouth and bit into it as it fell into her hungry mouth.

They walked round the edge of the zoo, until they came to the path that led past the back of the petting zoo. Isla was right – the fence was a bit lower there and they found a couple of logs and piled them up. It would take a huge leap to get in, but Isla told Heather she could do it and Heather scrunched nervously. She hid in a bush and agreed to wait until she heard Isla whistle three times from inside.

Isla thought about jumping over the fence herself, but it would have been breaking the law, and also she could see a man in the café on the other side, staring right at the spot where she'd land. She'd have to think of another way in. She gave Heather a pat and set off.

The moment she was out of sight of her friend her face fell. How on earth was she going to get herself inside, let alone a rather large pig? At that moment Isla had never felt more lost and alone. For a moment she thought of just running home and crawling under her duvet. Then she remembered Heather waiting for her patiently. Her friend had faith in her; she had to at least try.

When she got to the front of the zoo she saw a bus pull up that looked quite familiar. Where had she seen that bus before? As she was trying to place it, the door opened and Miss Stephenson stepped out onto the pavement! Of course, it was her old school bus – but what on earth was it doing here? She couldn't believe her eyes, as first Millie, then Tullynessle Morag, then Callum all got off the bus. Megan, Angus, Raj, Karen, Iain, even Jimmy Jamieson! Her whole class! In London! This was like a miracle. She wasn't alone; all her friends had come to help. She got up to go over and then . . .

'Miss Wolstenholme?'

She spun round to see Mr Hornbuckle, the weird pest control man, standing behind her. He looked rather gloomy. 'It *is* you. How . . . disappointing.'

Isla gulped. What was he doing here?

'My dog, Thomas, was following a smell. I often find it makes sense to let him follow a smell; you never know where it will lead. I had rather hoped he might be following that pig, Busby, but it seems he has led me to you instead.'

Isla gulped again. Minutes earlier and Heather would have been captured.

Mr Hornbuckle sighed. 'I suppose I might as well go for a walk, seeing as we're here. Thomas seems to want to go this way.'

He set off and headed straight towards the back of the zoo, right towards Heather's hiding place. She had to get Heather into the zoo. Fast! Isla spun around to see the last of her class heading through the barrier into the zoo. No! She'd missed them. She ran to where they'd gone in and shouted, but it was too late. They were inside and heading excitedly past the tigers.

'Can I help, dear?' asked the lady in the ticket office.

'That's my class! They've gone in without me!'

'It's funny, they didn't say there was anyone missing. They said thirty and that's how many I counted. Lovely group of children. Scottish. They won a competition to visit. Look.'

She held up a copy of the zoo newspaper which had the picture Miss Stephenson had taken on pet day with writing underneath: *London Zoo welcomes Old Meldrum School.*

Isla looked at the picture. 'That's me!' she said, pointing to the second row. 'Look, with the pig. Obviously I don't have the pig with me now but you can see it's me.'

The woman looked at the picture and then at Isla. 'It does look very like you, dear.'

'It is me! Please, before I lose them!'

The woman waved her through and Isla raced inside, looking around frantically to see where they'd gone.

There were zookeepers everywhere – cleaning, feeding, answering questions – and she ran up to one of them.

'Excuse me, have you seen a school party?'

The keeper nodded. 'They went that way. I think they were heading for the petting zoo.'

Isla ran as fast as she could go and, sure enough, just ahead she saw everyone stopped by the penguin pool being given instructions by Miss Stephenson.

Isla ran over to the fence and whistled three times. Heather's head popped out of the bush and snuffled at her happily.

'It's amazing. My class is here! You remember the photo we did on pet day? It won the competition and they're all here! It's how I got in. But we've got to get you in quick because Mr Hornbuckle's here as well! His dog followed your scent, but he thought it was me so he's walking around the outside. If the dog gets a sniff of you he'll find you, so we've got to get you in now. Can you climb up?'

As Heather shuffled up onto the logs, Isla looked around to check if the coast was clear. It seemed okay, but suddenly a green-sweatshirted zookeeper appeared and started explaining to some tourists about the difference between llamas and alpacas. She shooed Heather back into the bush, but as Heather climbed off the logs, they fell over and weren't in a nice pile any more. Meanwhile, the zookeeper was showing no signs of moving. Then Isla's heart stopped. Coming round the corner was Mr Hornbuckle, with Thomas by his side. And as she watched, Thomas lowered his nose to the ground, sniffed and then jerked his head up and barked once. He'd picked up Heather's scent!

Isla thought fast. She wasn't going to get this far and give up. She told Heather to stay where she was and ran towards the penguin pool. Miss Stephenson had finished talking and was leading everyone past the pigs towards the petting zoo. Isla grabbed Millie and pulled her aside.

'Millie, it's me.'

Her friend jumped out of her skin. 'Isla! What are you doing here?'

'I'll explain in a minute, but listen. Heather's in trouble and I really need your help.'

'Heather's here as well? I thought she was Busby now? Is she not?'

'Yes she is, but it's a long story.'

Out of the corner of her eye she could see Mr Hornbuckle being pulled along the path by Thomas, getting closer and closer to Heather by the second.

She looked at Millie in desperation. 'Will you help me? Please?'

Millie nodded. 'Of course. What do you want me to do?'

'I need a distraction. Can you get the others and make as much noise as you possibly can? I mean, like major, major noise?'

Millie grinned at her. 'You need some Old Meldrum mayhem? Leave it with me.' She ran off to the group and started whispering to them. The news spread like wildfire. 'Isla needs our help, we've to go wild!'

And go wild they did. London Zoo didn't know what had hit it. Suddenly it was like there were children everywhere. They ran, they shouted, they jumped, they yelled, they made mayhem. There was water going everywhere as Jimmy Jamieson turned on all the taps by the hand-washing place. There was straw going everywhere as Megan and Tullynessle

Morag grabbed the bedding out of the goats' bit of the petting zoo. There were chickens, goats and sheep running about all over the place as these farmers' children expertly freed the animals from their pens and got them running and jumping for all they were worth. The zoo staff were no match for this lot. They were blasting on their whistles and frantically running around, not knowing whether to control the animals or the children.

Isla watched in awe. She knew her friends could be mischievous, but this was better than she could have dreamt. She ran to the fence and whistled three times. Heather emerged from the bush, but as she did there were two short barks and suddenly Mr Hornbuckle spotted her. He started to run, his legs like long pistons while Thomas almost bounced along, his little legs whizzing. As they ran Mr Hornbuckle was shouting out, 'Busby! Stop! You're under arrest!'

'Come on, Heather!' shouted Isla, but now that the logs weren't piled up Heather was scared – the fence was too high! She was frozen.

Mr Hornbuckle reached under his jacket and

pulled out a length of rope. He whirled it like a proper cowboy, took aim and flung it lasso-like around the neck of the hunted pig. Once he reeled it in she'd be trapped.

Isla looked at her terrified friend, tears in both their eyes, and she willed her to make one last try. 'Jump, Heather, jump!' whispered Isla.

Heather backed up six paces, took a deep breath, gathered herself and then took a run up. With a mighty heave, she took off, soaring through the air and sailing towards the fence into the zoo. As she flew, Mr Hornbuckle dug his heels in and prepared to pull her back, but Heather was too strong and as she flew over the fence he was yanked off his feet. The rope slipped out of his hands and he flew headfirst into a huge muddy puddle, just as the pig he'd been chasing landed right in the middle of a bush just inside the fence.

Chapter 16

Pigs
Do Migrate

Millie and her friends were still creating an amazing diversion, but they were tiring and Isla knew they only had minutes to get Heather to safety. She shoved Heather into one of the play huts and went in with her. Heather was gasping for breath and Isla gave her a massive hug.

'I'm so proud of you, but we don't have any time.

These pigs live in the open, and there's nowhere for you to hide. We've got to get to the Bearded pigs' enclosure. It's just over there – the big green building with loads of rocks.'

She stuck her head out just in time to see two keepers trying to grab Iain as he ducked and dived. He seemed to have got an ice cream from somewhere and was using it to get a sheep to charge between the two keepers, knocking them completely off balance. She grinned and looked round. The coast was clear so she grabbed Heather and set off.

As they moved, Isla kept talking. 'I think you'll be fine with the Bearded pigs. The information board says they're mostly from South Asia – that's places like China and Borneo and Sumatra and so on. Their piglets are striped when they're born, and they have yellow tufts of hair around their snouts, which is why they're called Bearded pigs. They have quite thin bodies but massive heads and they eat anything.'

They got to the pig enclosure safely and dropped down out of sight. Isla turned to Heather.

'Right, I'll help you over this trench and then

you're on your own. I think you'll just have to blend in as best you can. I'll come and see you as soon as possible, so keep an eye out for me. That pest man knows you're in here so you'll have to stay out of sight, but you'll be fine. Hopefully they'll stop looking for you, and I can convince Dad to let you come and live with us, but that might take a while.'

They waited until nobody was around and then Isla knelt down. Heather very gently scrambled up on her back and jumped across the trench into the pig enclosure. She landed and turned to face Isla. Suddenly it hit both of them. This was goodbye again. Isla put her hands across the moat and gently stroked Heather's snout. Heather snickered and then lowered her head and shook it from side to side until the coin on the string fell off. She picked it up in her mouth and held it out to Isla. Isla didn't trust herself to speak so she just took the coin, hung it around her own neck and reached back to stroke her friend one more time.

'Oi! Get your hand out of the enclosure!'

Isla looked round to see a zookeeper in a green

uniform waving and running towards her. She bent down, blew Heather a kiss and spoke very quickly. 'You'd better run inside and hide for a bit until you know what to do and you've made friends. I'll come and visit you, I promise. I'll whistle three times.'

Heather scampered off and Isla stood up as the zookeeper arrived, slightly out of breath.

'You must be careful, young lady. Some of these animals can give you a nasty bite. Best not try to touch them. If you want to do that there's the petting zoo over there. It's just behind the penguin pool.' He looked around. 'Are you here with the school? They were making a real noise but I think they've calmed down now.'

Isla nodded, but there was something she had to know. 'Excuse me, are the Bearded pigs friendly? I mean, to other pigs?'

The man looked at her curiously. 'What an interesting question. I'm not sure if they are what you would call friendly, but they are the only pigs in the world who actually migrate. That means every winter a big group of them travels hundreds of miles to find food. Zebras and wildebeest do it in Africa, lots of birds migrate, but these are the only pigs in the world that do it. And they always do it in a big herd so I imagine they must like being together. Does that answer your question?'

Isla was grinning. 'Thank you, that's great.'

A phone started to ring somewhere as she headed off towards the petting zoo. She walked along and thought to herself that the zookeeper was wrong. There was another type of pig who migrated. Duroc pigs. They came from Scotland to London.

The phone was still ringing and she could feel a tingling in her pocket. She reached in and felt something vibrating. Eek! It was the phone her dad had given her, and it was ringing!

Isla answered her phone tentatively. 'Hello?'

'Hi love. Did I wake you?'

It was her dad. She hated lying to her dad. She took a deep breath. 'No.'

'Good. Are you in bed?'

Isla looked round her. 'No.'

'Oh great, so you're feeling better?'

'Yes,' said Isla decisively, relieved she hadn't actually had to lie yet.

'Good, that's good. I'll be home in five minutes so I'll see you then.'

Ouch.

'Well, I'm, um, sort of, um, not quite . . . actually at home . . .'

There was a long pause from her dad.

'I see. And where exactly are you?'

'Don't go nuts, but I'm sort of at . . . um—'

'The zoo? By the spider monkeys?' interrupted her dad.

Isla looked at the phone in disbelief. How did he know?

She turned around and there, standing right behind her, was Mr Wolstenholme. He looked absolutely furious as he grabbed Isla and hugged her impossibly tight.

'Don't ever do that to me again! Why are you here? Where have you been? I love you so much! I'm so cross. I couldn't bear to lose you as well. You're grounded for ever.'

The energy that had got Isla this far finally ran out and everything that had been bottled up inside her overflowed and came out in a torrent of words.

'Please don't be cross, I just missed her so much and I'm trying to be grown-up and make living here work, but it's really hard and I couldn't talk to anyone, and then I saw all my old class and I really miss them and Miss Stephenson, and they're so nice and do you think Millie could stay for a sleepover?'

Her dad looked utterly baffled, so Isla grinned at him.

'My school. Old Meldrum. They won the competition and they're all here. Come and say hi.'

She led him to where Miss Stephenson was telling the children off more than she ever had before. The trouble was that she was trying not to laugh as she did it, so the effect was slightly spoilt.

'Dad, wait here a sec, there's something I've got to do.' She walked over to Miss Stephenson and tugged at her hand.

'Isla!' exclaimed the teacher. 'What on earth are you doing here?' Then she looked suspicious. 'Was this something to do with you? The chaos, I mean?'

Isla nodded. 'Miss Stephenson, please don't be cross with them. I asked them to help out and make mayhem. They were only doing what I asked, so if you're going to punish anyone it should be me.'

The teacher looked disapproving. 'That explains it. May I ask why?'

'I'm afraid I can't tell you, but it was in a very good cause, I promise. Can Millie come for a sleepover? Please?'

Miss Stephenson laughed. 'I'm afraid not. We're going home today so we'll be leaving after lunch, but well done for owning up. I admire your honesty and I'm glad to see London hasn't changed you too much.'

The teacher looked around at the happy zoo animals and the exhausted keepers. 'I don't think they'll forget Old Meldrum in a hurry, but no real harm seems to have been done. Will you come back and visit us soon? Maybe you can tell us about your pig Heather and her rise to fame?'

Isla nodded and waved goodbye to all her class. Then she walked off with her dad.

'Dad?'

'Yes.'

'How did you find me? Today, I mean?'

'That phone I left you with. It's got a special thing on it that shows me where you are. I didn't look until I was about to leave work and when I did and it said you were at the zoo I nearly had a fit! So I came straight over and called you when I got here.'

'I'm glad you did.'

'Me too. So why are we here? I mean, I know why I'm here, but why are you here?'

Isla looked at her dad. 'Can I ask you an if?'

'You haven't done that for ages. They're called hypothetical questions, by the way.'

'If you had a friend and she was really in trouble but to help you had to do something you knew was wrong, what would you do?'

The farmer looked thoughtfully at his daughter. 'I might think what kind of trouble could be so bad that I couldn't tell someone.'

'If it wasn't like naughty, bad trouble, but trouble like she was in danger trouble?'

'Same answer.'

'But they were going to kill her and she's not mad, she was just trying to find me and she didn't mean to bite silly Anaya Postlethwaite, although she deserves it because she's mean to everyone, but she was just looking for me and then I couldn't have let her be killed, and she trusted me and now she's safe and you can punish me all you like, but I'm never going to say I'm sorry for what I did. Except for lying to you and making you worried. I'm really sorry about that.'

She looked at the ground with her arms folded in front of her and her brow scrunched up into a mixture of guilty and cross.

Her dad looked at her. 'Okay. Shall we go home then?'

'Are you not going to punish me?'

'Should I?'

'But I went across London on my own! I didn't tell Mrs Maatens!'

'Yes. I wonder if she's noticed you're missing yet?'

'Dad!'

'Actually, I'm rather proud of you. I'm not saying I

wasn't worried sick, and if you ever do it again, I'll take away everything – including your legs – so you have to stay in one place, but you obviously had what you considered to be a very good reason. I might not agree with you, and I might think you'd have been better off telling me about it, but you made a choice and you acted on it. And that makes me proud. And you travelled all the way across this massive city all on your own. That's impressive.'

They were just passing the front entrance to the zoo and Isla saw Mr Hornbuckle approaching the ticket office with Thomas waddling along behind him. He tried to march straight in, but the man stopped him.

'It's twenty-five pounds to come in, sir, and I'm afraid there are no pets allowed.'

Mr Hornbuckle was sore from his tangle with Heather, he was extremely grubby, his glasses were wonky and he was feeling rather embarrassed and very short of patience.

'I don't think you understand. There's an escaped pig inside the zoo. My job is to find her, and my dog is the only way to do it. So, if you will just allow us to go in, we'll say no more about this.'

'An escaped pig?'

'Yes. Busby the pig. She's in the zoo.'

'Busby the pig? In the zoo?'

'Yes. She jumped over the fence while I was distracted.'

The man in the kiosk looked at him disbelievingly.

'She jumped? Over the fence? While you were distracted?'

'Stop repeating everything I say and let me in. I have to catch a pig!'

The man picked up the phone by his side. 'Security? Can you come to kiosk four? I've got a nutter here who needs to be removed. Yes, quite mad, I'm afraid.'

Isla was grinning and her dad looked down at her thoughtfully.

'I wonder what he was doing here? I think I'd better buy a season ticket for the zoo. Something tells me we may be spending quite a lot of time here.'

Isla linked her arm through his and gave him the

biggest grin she had. In the background, Mr Hornbuckle was being dragged away by the zoo security guards, still shouting, 'She's in there! She's inside! You must believe me!'

Back in the enclosure, Heather yawned. She was tired after all her adventures and wanted nothing more than to lie down and think about nothing at all for a week. She'd found an apple on the ground and she was puzzled that it was a variety she didn't know. Tasty though, and she munched on it contentedly, thinking happily about things as she did so.

So much had happened since the barn had burnt down. She was miles away from home, in a strange place, surrounded by amazingly exotic animals she didn't know, but somehow she wasn't scared or nervous. She didn't even mind that her head was full of thoughts. After all, they were good thoughts: she was in the same place as her best two-legged friend, she was safe, there were apples on the trees and somehow, even though she had no idea what tomorrow might bring, for now, she was happy. That reminded her of something that Isla had scribbled in her spidery writing on the wall of the barn a long time ago. She'd called it her recipe for a happy Heather.

A sleep in the morning
          and an apple for lunch,
    if that sounds like a plan,
          then give me a scrunch.

Heather scrunched.

Heather's Apple Alphabet

A is for *Alderman*, good to cook and eat
B is for *Braeburn*, crunchy and sweet
C is for *Cox's Pippin*, sharp, crisp and green
D is for *Dog's Snout*, tastes of ice cream
E is for *Earliblaze*, tart and cherry-red,
F is for *Flower of Kent*, that fell on Newton's head
G is for *Glockenapfel*, shaped just like a bell
H is for the *Herring's Pippin*, and its amazing smell
I's the *Irish Peach*, needs eating fast, it will not keep
J is for *Jazz*, tastes of peardrops and is loved by sheep
K's the *Kentish Fillbasket*, the biggest apple you can find
L is for *Lady Henniker*, delicate, subtle, quite refined
M's the mighty *Mountain Boomer*, cooks to a sticky paste

N's the **_New Rock Pippin_**, with its funny liquorice taste
O's the stripy **_Orkney_**, grown in Scotland by the sea
P's the **_Polish Papiérowka_**, which tastes of lightly sugared-tea
Q is for **_Queen Cox_**, ever so easy to grow
R is for **_Ribston Pippin_**, with flesh like sweetened snow
S is for the noble **_Spartan_**, red and crisp and clean
T is for **_Tydeman's Red_** whose flesh is weirdly green
U's for the Swiss **_Uttwiler Spätlauber_** to keep you looking young
V's the **_Viking_**, its attacking flavour is acidic on your tongue
W's the **_Westfield Seek-No-Further_**, that's crisp, if rather plain
X in **_Goikoetxea_** shows it's Basque, from Northern Spain
Y's the **_Yorkshire Goosesauce_**, oldest apple of them all
Our final apple's **_Zari_**, which is sweet but rather small.

Now you know Heather's apple alphabet.

She's eaten every one of these apples, and many more besides.

How many of them have you tried?

PRESS

Thank you for choosing a Piccadilly Press book.

If you would like to know more about our
authors, our books or if you'd just like to know
what we're up to, you can find us online.

www.piccadillypress.co.uk

You can also find us on:

We hope to see you soon!